In **Part 1**, Cyril Fothergill stumbles upon an evil plot that could destroy the world by plague. With the blessing of the British prime minister, Cyril and his trusted cohort, Geoffrey Cowlishaw, travel to Italy. . . to a top-secret meeting with Pope Adolfo I. On the way, Cyril and Geoffrey witness a dramatic self-sacrifice.

In **Part 2**, Cyril and Geoffrey discover the greatest obstacle to their top-secret mission: Baldasarre Gervasio, the pope's most trusted advisor, reviled as the "ratman." After Cyril discovers Gervasio's secret "experiments," he is followed into Gervasio's underground kingdom—the Roman catacombs—by a horde of trained rats who wait only for their master's command.

In **Part 3**, after a miraculous escape from the catacombs, Cyril begins his journey home to England, accompanied by Henry Letchworth. Signs of a sinister betrayal abound as the two men are shipwrecked and encounter a group of Druids bent on their destruction.

In **Part 4**, as the horrors of an ancient cult—thought to be eradicated but clearly thriving—come to light, Cyril must find the way of escape before it is too late. Trapped in an underground maze, he finds himself at the mercy of a traitor—none other than the Lord Geoffrey Cowlishaw.

In **Part 5**, the long-dreaded virus has been unleashed. As the world collapses around them, Sarah and Clarice Fothergill must find a way to survive. As they begin a journey that they pray will take them back home to England, their only hope is in their Heavenly Father.

*Now, Roger Elwood's
riveting six-part adventure
concludes with. . .*

PART 6
BRIGHT PHOENIX

A RIVETING SIX-PART ADVENTURE

PART 6
WITHOUT THE DAWN

BRIGHT PHOENIX

ROGER
ELWOOD

BARBOUR
PUBLISHING, INC.
Uhrichsville, Ohio

© MCMXCVII by Roger Elwood

ISBN 1-57748-043-0

Published by Barbour Publishing, Inc.
          P.O. Box 719
          Uhrichsville, Ohio 44683
          http://www.barbourbooks.com

ecpa Member of the
Evangelical Christian
Publishers Association

Printed in the United States of America.

CHAPTER 1

Midnight. . . .

The soldiers were asleep except for those assigned to guard duty. Their current duty had been uneventful so far, though the potential of something going haywire was always there, especially as Europe seemed ever closer to collapse in the midst of a destructive and pervasive epidemic.

Something going haywire. . . .

That moment finally arrived a few seconds after midnight under, perhaps coincidentally, the brightest full moon anyone could remember seeing in a long time.

Louis Dafoe, after standing guard only a few moments, suddenly realized he was covered with perspiration.

Someone was screaming so loudly that virtually everybody else in the fortress was awakened. But it was the French soldiers who reacted first, trained as they were to be ready in an instant, all of their senses functioning optimally.

"Sounds like the devil himself is dragging somebody right to hell!" one of the men said. He was interrupted by a second scream that was, if anything, louder than the first.

And another after that.

Captain Dafoe listened, trying to detect the source.

"It's not inside!" he exclaimed. "But where?"

"The woods!" a sergeant said, pointing.

They all looked where he was directing their attention.

Light. . . .

Like dancing flames. Sinister flames. The nearby wooded area was being burnt down to embers.

"Fire!" another soldier shouted.

As he saw the pulsating light, Dafoe ordered fifteen of the men to stay at the fortress.

"Half of you outside," he said. "The others go inside and see if anything is happening. Do not leave until I tell you."

And then he and five soldiers started walking toward the woods. As soon as they entered, Dafoe could feel his nerve ends tingling.

"It should be warm," he said, "but it is not. So cold!" *Almost freezing. . . .*

"Like the chill of a tomb!" one of the other men agreed, his teeth starting to chatter. "I have never felt anything like it, Captain, except in a graveyard."

The flames were directly ahead of them, fragments of color reaching past the branches and leaves and touching their bodies in an almost surreal kaleidoscope.

And an odor.

Dafoe and the others had smelled it before when men and women were caught in a building set ablaze by terrorists.

Finally they entered a clearing.

The six men approached with great caution and saw what none of them could have conceived was possible.

Flames, yes, but not of wood burning.

Half a dozen human beings had been hung on makeshift crosses, reminiscent of two thousand years earlier, those cruel Roman times.

One of the soldiers gasped, stuttering, "Who c–c–could be responsible for this horror?"

There, sitting out of range of the flames, were a dozen children, possibly between the ages of twelve and fifteen, watching, clapping their hands gleefully as they heard the agonizing moaning.

"This is better than I thought it would be!" one of them said, his enthusiasm not hidden. "What a cool idea!"

It was apparent from the expressions of the others that the lot of them could not have agreed more.

Dafoe's mind briefly flashed back to something he had seen in a pet store years earlier: A snake was being fed a live white mouse. Several children had been sitting in front of the waterless tank where this was happening.

"Cool!" one of them had said as the mouse struggled to get free while making pitiable squeaking sounds.

After that one mouse was consumed, the children had begged the store manager to feed the snake another one.

Dafoe, who was just out of his teens then, stepped forward and berated the manager, demanding that the "show" be stopped.

"It's an education," was the other man's response.

"An abomination!" Dafoe countered. "You're celebrating death. You're—"

"Out of my store!"

Dafoe had left but returned with a policeman who had agreed it was too ghoulish for the youngsters to be allowed to watch.

"But it happens several times a day," the manager professed. "I used to have one store where I had some baby sharks. They needed to be fed several times a day. I posted the schedule, and you know, people would start coming just to watch."

"You will stop immediately!" the officer demanded.

"This is life," the owner insisted. "Is it not?"

"No, sir, it is death. Death should never be something enjoyed by spectators. You are teaching them to appreciate this sort of thing. How many will grow up having no respect for animals as a result? How many will begin torturing innocent creatures?"

What Dafoe was seeing now in that clearing—children enjoying the death of adults—was an ungodly image reminiscent of those others who had enjoyed the sight of a defenseless white mouse being swallowed whole by a snake.

"Be ready. . ." he whispered to the other soldiers.

He waited a few seconds, then they followed him into

the clearing.

"Why have you done this?" he demanded.

No one on the crosses seemed to be alive; even if any of them were alive but merely unconscious, there was no chance they could survive much longer.

The children all jumped to their feet.

One boy stepped forward, an exaggerated sneer on his face.

"What's wrong with it?" he asked emotionlessly.

Startled, Dafoe knew then that he would never again be amazed by what awful acts human beings could perpetrate.

"You do not seem concerned that you have murdered six people," he said.

"Executed," the boy retorted. "The law would not assume the responsibility. We had no choice."

"Who found them guilty?"

"We did."

"You? A court of mere young people! No legal authority would accept your verdict. Surely you realize that."

"It's why we acted on our own."

"For what reason?"

The boy turned to the others.

"Show him," he told them.

Scars and fresh bruises and, in one case, an eye socket with an obvious and rather grotesque glass eye stuck in it.

"Our parents did this to us," the boy added. "It's payback time, and not a day too soon!"

He pointed over the shoulders of the men.

"Yeah, here, and back there!" he shouted.

"But you can't just—" Dafoe began to say rather lamely.

"We have allies this time," the boy growled. "The forces of darkness listened to us when the church would not."

Knives. . . .

In an instant all of the children produced knives that they had been hiding.

"You do not want to do this," Dafoe warned them. "Put the weapons away, and we will forget that you have them."

"Wrong!" their leader screamed with a ferocity none of the soldiers had ever seen from one so young.

The young boys then started throwing the knives.

Repelled by what he must do, Dafoe nevertheless had no choice but to open fire, his men doing the same.

Eight of the children died instantly, no match for the government forces. Others were wounded and started to crawl away into the woods.

"Stop!" Dafoe pleaded. "We will help you."

They paid no attention and were out of sight in seconds.

Only one of the knives had found a target, the left arm of one of the soldiers. A comrade pulled it out expertly, but the pain made the man lose consciousness, and he had to be carried by the others.

"Now we must mow down children. . ." Louis Dafoe muttered. "We'll come back and bury them in the morning."

"What about the bodies on those crosses?" another man asked.

The flames had started to die down.

"They're dead," Dafoe observed. "We'll bury them as well."

"What has happened to our children, Captain?" the same soldier speculated.

"I think—"

But his voice wavered.

"Yes, Captain?"

"I think their lives have been cheapened for a long time. . ." Dafoe said slowly. "It began in America with unborn babies sacrificed on the altar of *Roe v. Wade*."

As he visibly shivered from the images presenting themselves in his mind, the other soldier nodded sadly.

"Disposable, Captain," he muttered. "Pop them in a trash bag and throw them away."

Dafoe ordered the men back to the fortress. As they approached, one of those left behind to guard the huge structure came running toward Dafoe.

"Inside, sir!" he babbled.

"What's inside?" the captain asked.

"It started a few minutes ago then stopped for a while."

"What are you talking about?"

"Crazy things. . .people screaming about demons and ghastly screeching sounds, enough to freeze the blood, Captain."

For a moment Dafoe listened but could detect nothing except the normal sounds of nighttime animals.

Then—

. . .people screaming. . .ghastly screeching sounds.

Suddenly they heard, coming from inside the fortress, the awful cacophony of people being driven over the edge of madness.

CHAPTER 2

The soldiers burst into the fortress, ready with their guns and knives. What they saw seemed to most of them like a scene from some medieval representation of hell.

Berserk.

People were running in every direction, screaming, shouting such awful obscenities that even the soldiers flinched.

Most were bleeding from cuts or gashes on their cheeks, necks, shoulders, and other parts of their bodies.

"They are mad!" one soldier said.

"No," Louis Dafoe told him, "they are possessed."

"We are rational men, we cannot—"

"That is why I said what I did. It is the only *rational* explanation."

Dafoe was correct. Since most of the people in the so-called fortress were not Christians, they were subject to demonic control, even possession.

Suicides were attempted, and many succeeded, men and women slitting their wrists, stabbing themselves in the chest, or putting the barrel of a pistol—

A night of violence and death.

Without those who were Christians, without the monks and several ministers staying inside, the toll would have been higher.

Finally it was stopped, and the demonic entities were banished by a Christ-centered counterattack of prayer and the forged-together faith of longtime believers and those who converted that night. . .

The next morning at breakfast there was more conversation than usual but of a nervous sort, with startling experiences being exchanged over and over, some new details remembered and repeated for the benefit of avid listeners who were ready with their own stories to tell.

As guests took their place at the long, heavy table in the main banquet room and ate the generous meal placed before them, they also half-expected another demonic attack, either inflicted upon one of them or perhaps upon the entire group within the fortress.

A middle-aged man moaned as he sat at one of the half-dozen long tables in the banquet hall. "We made it through this last time, but who knows about the next?"

"But you should be saying something that you are not," the much younger man sitting to his left offered.

"And what is that?"

"You neglected to use one word."

"What. . ."

The younger man paused for effect then continued, *"If,* and, I emphasize that is a very big *if,* there should be another attack. Who can say? We are here now talking to one another, and none of us was directly involved. Can you be certain that someone else is a target or that all of us are?

"Does that not prove something?" he continued. "And what about gratitude? Are we not inviting catastrophe if we remain so fearful instead of telling Christ Jesus that we are His and His only through the rest of our lives and on into eternity? We have had here, until now, what we did not have on the outside: security. If that must end now, so be it. But we should not be ungrateful for the weeks or months that we did feel safe, blessed as they were."

And so it went throughout the hall.

For Clarice and Sarah, it was different.

What with dozens of people seated, and with the aroma of food apparent, it all seemed so familiar to the two sisters, reminding them both of breakfasts back home when guests from the previous day had stayed over and joined them.

So much like we once enjoyed, Clarice thought. *Oh, the banquets we used to have, the laughing, the music, the—*

Gone.

She realized, with the greatest sorrow of her young life, that everything she and her sister had ever enjoyed was gone, more than likely for all time. Even if they were fortunate enough to return home safely, they had no way of knowing what they would face upon arriving at the castle. What would be left of their family? With Cyril Fothergill quite possibly a victim of demonic assault and their mother surely dead, as much from her condition as from concern for her beloved, they might return to an immense, empty castle.

"You must not bloody yourself," Sarah said, breaking into her thoughts. "That would upset them, you know."

"Bloody myself?" Clarice repeated. "What do you mean?"

"Tormenting yourself with what might be happening or has already happened to Mother and Father, and blaming yourself for not being there at their side."

"You are surely doing the same, Sarah."

Their closeness since they were children had made them much like identical twins, closely attuned to one another's thoughts.

"I am," Sarah acknowledged. "But it is wrong, and I know that. They would want us to think of no one but ourselves, because in doing that, we concentrate on getting back home, not on what will greet us when we get there. We must not let ourselves become sloppy."

. . .to think of no one but ourselves.

In another context Clarice might have been appalled by what her sister had said, but under the circumstances, she did grasp Sarah's point. If they kept confronting the fact over and over, morning, afternoon, and evening, that their mother and their father both were dead and buried, the two of them could quickly become dispirited, wondering what the point was of returning to Fothergill Castle. The castle had once been an oasis of safety, defended by former bobbies who had pledged their loyalty to the Fothergills long before, but those men were now helpless before an invasion by an enemy that none of them could stop.

With their loved ones gone, wiped out by the ravages of the hantavirus or dead of some other affliction, as they fully anticipated was the case with Elizabeth Fothergill, would they be reduced to simply wandering through the cold, empty hallways of their once magnificent home, propelled by their grief into early graves of their own?

"I cannot bear to look where she is buried," Clarice said. "I cannot bear to know that I was not able to be with her when it happened, to hold her hand for whatever comfort that might have been. I cannot bear to stand by her grave and know I was not able to attend her funeral and kiss her forehead one last time."

"Poor Mother was so frail when we left her," Sarah recalled. "I felt that when I held her in my arms. I had to be so careful, so careful, Clarice, because I did not want to fracture or break any of her bones."

Someone tapped Clarice on the shoulder.

A blond-haired woman, thirtyish, with deep lines on a face possessed with a toughness that made her seem much older.

"I hope you are not annoyed, but I overheard a bit of what you have been saying," she remarked. "Would you consider it obnoxious if I were to say something about those concerns of yours?"

"Go ahead," Clarice told the woman. "But first, tell us your name."

"Monique Dumelle," she replied.

"Why are you here?" Sarah asked.

"I am accused of being a sorcerer's apprentice," Monique acknowledged, "a witch. For a time, I worked at the Vatican."

Monique had been speaking louder than she intended, and her words were picked up by others at the same table and throughout the banquet hall.

"I was very close to Baldasarre Gervasio, a priest stationed at the Vatican," Monique went on to tell Clarice and Sarah, knowing that his name was no longer as little known as it had been a few years before and that the very mention of it would generate a sharp reaction from anyone who was at all aware of his role in the epidemic.

Neither of the sisters surprised her by their response, which was unveiled astonishment.

"In fact, I was his mistress," she added quickly.

Utensils were dropped, stunned reactions could be heard, and angry voices raised.

"You—" Clarice immediately stopped herself, the thought of spending a night or many nights with such a man causing a wave of revulsion inside her.

"Slept with the ratman?" Sarah, who was equally nauseated, managed to say.

"Yes. . . ." Monique admitted.

She seemed to find their reactions amusing as a slight grin curled up the edges of her rather large mouth.

"Well, what is a girl to do, you know?" she asked almost blithely while Clarice and Sarah cringed.

Having heard enough of this dialogue, several people at other tables had gotten to their feet and were starting to walk toward her, but Monique Dumelle seemed oblivious to everyone except Clarice and Sarah.

"But why are you here?" Clarice asked. "If you were so close to Gervasio, why have you decided to run away?"

Monique's eyelids shot wide open.

"My life is in danger. . ." she muttered.

Clarice found this a strange admission. Although the

fortress had not stopped the entry of demonic creatures, the
massive structure was surely impregnable to possible human
invasion by those who might be after Monique Dumelle.

"For what reason? There are guards outside. And these
walls must be reassuring. Monique, you are as safe as the rest
of us. Why are you worried?"

"Gervasio wants me dead. And Gervasio is accustomed
to getting what he demands."

Clarice was becoming confused.

"Why would he want his mistress murdered?"

"Because of certain documents."

"What documents?"

"Secret communiqués to some people in the Middle East."

"Terrorists?"

"Yes, Muslim terrorists. These documents did not have
Gervasio's signature. And rather than use someone inside the
Vatican to write each one, he brought in from the streets of
Rome men who could be paid off and then could slip forgotten back into the masses—or be murdered perhaps—Gervasio
was careful about that sort of thing—but what was written
clearly showed that there was a traitor within the Vatican."

"Who got the documents?" Sarah asked.

Monique's broad grin was filled with irony.

"Pope Adolfo himself," she announced.

"For anything of that sort to happen, how could it be
someone other than Gervasio himself who became as careless as that? He must have reached such a level of arrogance
that made him think he was invincible."

"I have to agree," Monique said, appreciating Sarah's
astuteness.

"But why are you the object of Gervasio's vengeance?
It would seem that he could not be bothered."

"By a witch-woman of the night, you mean?"

"To be honest, yes."

"Very simply this: He turned me in," Monique remarked.

"As far as Gervasio was concerned, I became a handy scape-goat, directing attention away from him. But I managed to escape, thanks to some favors from, shall we say, old friends in the priesthood."

"Yet Adolfo surely must have understood that you alone could not have been responsible for all the conspiracies and whatever else those documents—"

Monique interrupted her.

"Gervasio told Adolfo that I had sold myself out to the enemy, that I was the traitor. And he brought in a cardinal to verify everything he said. He gave me credit for abilities I never knew I had."

For the first time Monique Dumelle seemed scared.

"Right now, I am in great danger," she said. "Gervasio's henchmen and spies from the pope's office are hunting for me."

She looked first at Clarice then at Sarah.

"I may be nothing more than a prostitute," she told them both, "but what I am *not* is one of Gervasio's treacherous conspirators. I fulfilled his lust and I was a link to the occult for him, and this was very wrong, yes, but I am in no way connected with the epidemic he has helped to bring upon the land."

"Then why did you spend time in his bed?" Sarah asked. "If you knew what he was doing, how could you stand it? The thought of having the ratman touch me—!"

She felt so unclean just imaging such a loathsome thing that taking a bath every hour for a month would not rid her of that feeling.

"I have to be honest," Monique Dumelle replied. "Baldasarre Gervasio did pay me well. . .money and jewels, for one thing. . .and he sent me on fascinating trips to different countries and to islands in the Mediterranean.

"And again, he knew of no other prostitutes who were also witches and no other witches who were also prostitutes."

"Why was it so important that you be a witch?" Clarice asked.

"I could help him with the ceremonies he conducted in the catacombs. I already knew the words."

"The ceremonies? The words? What are you talking about?"

"I must not say. They were so awful, so blasphemous. I think God would strike me dead if I tainted your mind with them."

"Or is it that you think I would not believe you?"

"I know you believe me. That is the problem. What I witnessed, what I helped with, was no less than a scene from hell."

Monique Dumelle would never be free of the images, unholy rites conducted over the remains of Christians, unspeakable acts committed with their bones, acts so foul they could not be described to anyone.

And that one night, when the fabric between mortal life, finite life, and Satan's netherworld was torn asunder and she could see demons—

"I lived it all," Monique declared, trying hard to cast the memories from her mind.

"And all this without Pope Adolfo's knowledge?"

"Always. Anyone who found out was murdered before the pope could be alerted."

"Why not go back? Place yourself at Adolfo's mercy. Get protection."

The people who had stood and were walking toward Monique Dumelle now surrounded the table at which she was sitting.

"She must be the one responsible for what happened earlier," one man said. "It was through her that the demons gained entrance."

Mutterings broke out.

For a moment, Clarice and Sarah thought that Monique

could not escape being dragged from that large banquet hall and perhaps killed by what would become a frenzied, vengeance-driven mob or face injury and banishment from what was supposed to have been a place of refuge similar to the cities of refuge detailed in the Old Testament. But in biblical times the protection promised had been from those on the outside, not dangerous antagonists within.

Another voice, a more authoritative one, drowned out everyone else.

A determined Brother Thaddeus, with Brother Nathaniel right next to him, now strode into the large dining hall.

"As of last night, I can report with considerable joy that Monique Dumelle here has become a Christian, as have many of you, I trust. Furthermore, and most courageously, she has agreed to return to the Vatican as soon as humanly possible and tell what she knows about the unholy plan of that devil named Baldasarre Gervasio."

Many of the guests scoffed at this.

"Pope Adolfo would never believe anything that spewed forth from the painted, contaminated lips of a common tramp such as this one," one of the women shouted. "Her efforts, assuming she could do this at all, would be to no avail; her mission would achieve nothing more than wasting the time of everyone who was involved."

"Oh, but the holy father will listen," Brother Nathaniel spoke, "if Brother Thaddeus and I both tell him we believe Monique Dumelle."

Impulsively, Clarice stood, as did Sarah.

"As we shall do also," she said. "Adolfo is well aware of our father. That alone will gain his attention."

A waspy little man got to his feet.

"Who are you?" he asked, wagging a finger at them.

"The daughters of Cyril and Elizabeth Fothergill."

There had been increased murmuring until the two sisters stood. But after Clarice identified herself and her sister there was only a hushed silence.

Finally that same little man stepped forward.

"I am very sorry," he said. "I knew your father. I did business with him. He was an honorable man, a remarkably decent man."

. . .he was an honorable man, a remarkably decent man.

Both sisters should have been pleased by that comment, but it was his use of the past tense that startled them.

"You speak as though he is gone," Sarah said.

The man averted his eyes from her.

"You have not heard," he replied, sorry he had told her.

"Heard?" Clarice spoke this time. "Sir, what are you saying?"

He did not say anything for several seconds, struggling with what he knew.

"Cyril Fothergill is dead. . ."

Though the two sisters had tried to steel themselves for the eventuality that both parents were lost to them, they still carried the hope that they might be wrong.

. . .Cyril is Fothergill is dead.

Half of what they feared was now real.

. . .Cyril Fothergill is—

Clarice fell back against the table, her hands gripping the rough edges while she tried to steady herself. Sarah stood quietly as though she had not heard what was said, her face pale, emotionless.

Brother Thaddeus hurried up to Clarice and wrapped his long, thick arms gently around her thin waist.

"We shall go back to your quarters now," he said. "I am sure no one here is going to be foolish enough to stand in our way."

Brother Nathaniel did the same with Sarah who tried to push him away but without saying anything. Finally she fell into his arms and sobbed.

"Wait a minute!" said one of the women. "What about

this foul creature of the streets, this filthy—?"

Brother Nathaniel whispered something to Sarah, who nodded, and then he stepped back to face the one who had spoken.

"I find you, madam, more repugnant than Monique Dumelle, of whom you speak so unfeelingly," he said loud enough that even Clarice, faint as she was, could scarcely believe what he was saying.

"That creature is a witch by her own admission, and she is also a call girl!" the woman added. "You are a man of God. How can you tear into me like that and ignore her? I am a God-fearing citizen."

"Do you know anything else about her?"

"I know she has engaged in incantations and ceremonies that are an abomination. What more is there to know?"

"Right now you are as much of a sinner as she. You have judged her first and shown no interest in finding out anything else about her. You have decided, while knowing little or nothing of her life, that she is guilty, and I suspect, according to you, Monique Dumelle is more than worthy of death by stoning."

Another man then stepped in front of the woman.

"I am Hans Galanis," he bellowed, his eyes bloodshot. "How dare you talk to my wife, Marie, in that manner!"

Angered and insulted, he was clearly ready to strike a blow at a man of the cloth.

"I speak only as this woman you call your own deserves," Brother Nathaniel countered. "She is a reeking pool of deplorable ignorance. I find nothing in her attitude that is defensible, even by her husband!"

Galanis, probably outweighing the monk by fifty or more pounds, raised his fist and began swinging it forward. Brother Nathaniel gripped him around the wrist, bent the hand back, and forced Galanis to his knees.

"A few hours ago, Monique Dumelle got down on her

knees and had her sins forgiven by Christ Jesus. Will you be the one this day who disputes His eternal wisdom in now accepting her as one of His newly redeemed ones, whatever the gravity of her past sins, forgiven as these are through the shed blood of Jesus Christ?"

Galanis shook his head rapidly.

"Fine," Brother Nathaniel said, smiling as he released the other man. "Then my friends and I shall be on our way. I would be most grateful, Mr. Galanis, if you would step aside and let the five of us by."

But Monique did not go with them immediately. Instead, she decided to speak.

"The reason for the attack was my fault," she declared. "But not because I am the channel for any demons."

Few were prepared to believe her.

"Demons coming after one of their own, a common street witch?" Galanis protested disbelievingly. "That is nonsense. How can you expect us to swallow—?"

"Why should we take you at your word?" another shouted at her.

"Because of this," Monique said as she tore her blouse down the middle of her back and showed them her skin, keeping the front of her body covered.

Gashes.

Most of the women had to look away.

"I am not a flagellant; nor could I ever be one of their kind, though I have been known to consort, shall we say, with some of the less fanatical and dangerous ones from time to time," Monique explained. "But I suppose Gervasio, in that perverted little mind of his, thought he would do the flagellants a favor by handing me over—thinking they might someday owe him something in return—without any regard for me at all, this so-called *man* who once professed his love for me."

. . .*who once professed his love for me.*

For everyone else in that banquet hall, that statement had no real significance, but for Clarice and Sarah, it brought revulsion because they could not forget what their father had told them about the ratman.

Monique's cheeks were becoming red as she talked.

"I heard him tell several flagellants, 'Take your time. Monique Dumelle has many sins to be stripped away.' "

A collective gasp was heard when she said that, many men and women changing their attitudes toward Monique.

"So you did not summon the demons," Hans Galanis spoke hesitantly, his tone much softer, his manner bordering on being sympathetic. "Then why did you tell us you were the reason for what happened last night?"

"They were after me," she said. "That was why they came here. You see, I can do more damage than a hundred sturdy and well-armed men, damage where it would hurt the most. I know far too much. They tried as hard as they could to destroy me, but they failed."

Monique pointed to the two monks.

"Brother Thaddeus and Brother Nathaniel took this dirty body of mine, rank with all the sin I have committed, and they showed me how the Holy Spirit could wash it clean forever."

She looked from one person to another throughout the room.

"I felt clean for the first time since I was a child," she said. "None of you can even guess what it is like to have to get up each morning of each day of each week feeling ashamed of yourself but not being able to stop because no matter how disgusted you are, you have been doing what you do for so long that it has become a way of life."

Someone spat on the floor.

"I deserve that!" she exclaimed. "And believe me, I cannot but wonder why Almighty God, why my Creator—what a thought that is, to know that He knows me by name, that

He cares about me—is so willing, so eager to forgive my sins, to forget them as well and accept me as though I had never been sinning at all."

She pointed to the two monks.

"But according to what my new friends here told me, that is exactly His holy promise," she said exultantly, her joy unmistakable to the most cynical in that room.

Abruptly, Galanis's manner changed. He walked slowly up to her and looked at the wounds on her back.

"Some of these are so fresh," he said while he examined several. "They are still moist, sticky. They seem as though—"

Galanis took Monique's hand in his own because she seemed suddenly very weak. Softening the tone of his voice, he asked, "Last night? Some of these occurred last night, is that not it?"

Monique lowered her head.

"I am so ashamed," she said.

"You could not help what they did to you."

"They did not do it themselves."

Monique was shivering.

"They. . .forced me to cut away at my own body."

"You were not to able to stop?" Galanis inquired, not without sympathy. "They were too strong for you?"

"I did not have the blessed presence of the Holy Spirit within me then. I had only the most rancid memories of unspeakable evil and the most shameless yearnings, and I let them rule my life."

Monique knew that the crowd around her, if Galanis and his wife were examples, could never tolerate any description of the practices in which she had engaged as recently as two weeks earlier, and so she did not elaborate.

"I let occultic influences control me every minute of every day. In so many ways, even here, I was still one of their own, from all my years as a witch, and they knew this; they knew my weak spirit, and I had to obey their commands or be driven out of my mind."

Monique was crying by then.

"But here I am," she said. "I am patched up by my two new friends, friends I do not deserve. I suppose the good Lord above decided to step in and keep the demons at bay, at least for a while, silencing their voices in my very soul."

She chuckled ironically.

"And now I may never again be appealing to any man, with wounds that will surely become scars, disfiguring my body for the rest of my life. I am neither a witch nor a prostitute any longer. It really is something, you know, how this God of yours and mine goes about changing a life such as mine."

"What stopped them?" Galanis asked. "They were so close to destroying you."

"At first I fought against what they wanted. I told them I would no longer abuse myself. But this only infuriated them all the more. And then—"

She paused, closing her eyes, thinking of what happened next.

"I heard a voice in the hallway outside my room, and the sound of loud crying. It was a mother with her baby. The baby was crying, and she was trying to comfort him. The demons heard this also and were, I know, preparing to attack those two."

Her anguish was apparent to everyone who caught a glimpse of her face.

"I could not let this happen," she continued. "Nor could I allow them to hurt anyone else here. So I told them they could have every layer of skin, every muscle, every piece of bone, every drop of blood in my body if they would take just me and not hurt that poor mother and her little baby."

"But they did not attack you further, it seems. Why?" Galanis asked.

Brother Thaddeus cleared his throat.

"Let me answer for Monique since she may not be familiar with the theology of demons."

"She was willing to sacrifice herself for everyone here," he said. "Can you not grasp this? Can you not put your judgmental spirit aside for an instant? You certainly would not have done the same thing for her."

He glanced from Galanis to a woman near him and then to a man next to her and spotted others as well.

"Am I wrong?" he asked. "You thought of her only as the most deplorable sinner. How could you be expected to do anything so noble as that for her?"

Then he said, "The demons invading this supposedly invincible fortress saw a streak of pure goodness in an otherwise corrupt woman, and they could not cope. Just as darkness must flee light, so they could not remain before someone whose decency arose somehow in the midst of the foul life she had been leading.

"Monique became emboldened, throwing at them the handful of Bible verses to which she had been exposed during a more innocent time in her life. That was when Satan knew he had lost, for the time being anyway, for no life can expect to be freed of his attempts at spiritual seduction."

"So they just left?" Galanis asked, not quite willing to accept the simplicity of what the monk was saying.

"Monique told Brother Nathaniel and me that they were sucked from her room immediately after she spoke."

"Back into hell?"

"You are probably right. One of them shouted something at Monique about her sounding almost like a Christian. And then a wave of heat swept the room."

"Heat?" Marie Galanis queried.

"A wave of heat, yes, so intense that it seemed capable of melting anything in its path. But it was gone in an instant."

Others spoke of feeling oppressive heat that same night.

"I could almost smell the fire," a white-haired man with

a beautiful beard recalled.

Throughout the crowd voices arose, talking about identical experiences.

"I am deeply sorry," Galanis told Monique, his remorse unmistakable. "We do believe you, madam; we believe you now."

Monique Dumelle collapsed then and would have hit the floor if Hans Galanis had not hurried to catch her, holding her body with some awkwardness and knowing all too well that they both were under the gaze of all present in that banquet hall.

CHAPTER 3.

For Clarice and Sarah, news of their father's death brought with it the certainty that their mother must have died as well. They agreed that she could not survive her illness plus the shock of losing the only man who had ever been in her life. "That must have too hard for her," Clarice said. "She had little strength as it was. She had to have started going even more rapidly downhill. I can see her returning to his grave again and again, wishing they had died together."

"How awful. . ." Sarah remarked. "I was hoping they would be there to greet us, that when we came back, they would be given a new lease on life. But now—"

Clarice was angry.

"How selfish!" she screamed.

"No!" Sarah rebutted her. "You misunderstand. I thought we could help them, not the other way around. I would have given my own life for them if that could have helped."

Clarice hugged herself.

"Forgive me!" she pleaded. "I keep wondering if we are at fault."

"How could we be?"

"By going off, by not staying with them. I think Mother had some feeling about it, some kind of warning."

Clarice's teeth were audibly chattering. And Sarah also was feeling chilly, though not as much as her sister.

"I am so cold now," Clarice said. "I feel like somebody standing on an iceberg with no one else around. There is a terrible wind striking my face. It reaches through to my bones. I cannot stop it, Sarah. I am defenseless."

They had been outside, at the rear of the fortress, and stepped back in to get warm.

"I think Mother and Father lost hope when they did not hear from us," she continued. "They probably became convinced that we both had succumbed to the epidemic. Or to some other circumstance that just swallowed us up."

Her eyes were blood red.

"I can guess, oh, so clearly, how Father must have suffered from this. He would show so little emotion most of the time, I know, but it was only that he felt he had to keep his feelings hidden, not that he had none."

Tears were starting.

"With us taken from him and with Mother dying, I think the weight was too much for the man. No one has told us how Father died, but I can guess that it was his heart. It just stopped, weighed down by despair."

Her expression was peculiar.

"Those awful images. . ." she muttered. "Now this. Has God turned His back on us? Has He abandoned us?"

Even though her sister was by her side, Clarice felt completely alone.

"What will we do?" she asked, shedding her years of maturity and sounding like a frightened child. "They have been a part of us for more than twenty years. How do we just turn our backs on them? Can we ever do it, Sarah? Can we?"

That was the beginning for her.

Sarah at least had Louis Dafoe to turn to, however newfound their relationship, but Clarice was slipping quickly into depression.

Days later. . . .

"You know what I find most difficult?" Sarah told the young captain, needing to talk, to get her feelings out, to shun what was happening to her sister, a deterioration that threatened to destroy Clarice in a short span of time.

"Having no one to return to," he replied simply but powerfully.

She looked into his face, not aware that she was being transparent enough for him to guess as accurately as he did.

The emptiness. . . .

He was right, speaking with the kind of empathy that could only draw the two of them closer together.

"So many rooms and so many people and so much land and not a shilling's worth of debt, and yet it means little now."

She used to be reassured by the castle's presence. The walls were symbols of protection. As long as she remained behind them, she was safe. But when she returned, it would seem more like a tomb swallowing her up.

"I can understand your pain," Louis told her. "I just wish I could ease it."

"Being with you now helps," she said, "but I worry about my sister. She is here among strangers, and she will return to a house of hired help."

His arm around her waist, he pulled her closer to him.

"You are so warm," Sarah said after a bit.

"I was thinking the same about you," he told her. "I was thinking how wonderful it would be to hold you—"

She pressed a finger against his lips.

"Not yet," she said.

"You thought I was hinting at something with a purely carnal purpose."

She answered him by not answering at all.

"I do not think of you that way," he remarked, then realized what he had said and added, "I mean, not now, not for a while."

"But you are French, my dear Captain Louis," she teased him. "Should I have expected anything else?"

"I am French, yes, but I have a great deal of respect for

you, Sarah."

They had not heard the door open or the footsteps coming toward them.

"Captain!" another soldier said.

Young Dafoe sighed and turned to the other man.

"What is it?" he asked humorlessly.

"A messenger from the Vatican," the older soldier told him.

Sarah stepped forward.

"What did he want?" she asked.

"Pope Adolfo has agreed to see Monique Dumelle. And Baldasarre Gervasio is being confined to his quarters."

"Has the pope been told of Clarice and Sarah Fothergill?"

"He has, and he says they are welcome as well."

After the soldier left, Sarah and the young captain hugged one another.

"There might be hope!" she exclaimed. "And look! Here we are sharing it. The Lord is blessing us, Louis.

"You should be rejoicing," she told him, noticing that Louis was not exultant.

"I feel as you do, but with one difference."

"Tell me what it is."

"Getting hold of the culprits would be a victory. But the war can still be lost, even without their generals to manage the enemy's side."

"What do you mean, Louis?"

"The hantavirus is spreading. It wipes out thousands every week. The rats cannot be retrieved. They go their way, but even if they were stopped tomorrow, human beings themselves would ensure that the epidemic continues."

He paused, trying to smile reassuringly, but failed.

"Dear Sarah. . ." he said softly as he put his hands on her shoulders. "Capturing all the conspirators may make us feel good, but it will not change anything."

"So bleak. . ." she whispered. "So very bleak."

"But is it?" he spoke sternly. "Human beings survive. No one is saying that Europe will be destroyed altogether. There may be a million deaths—there may be ten million—but I cannot envision more than that. There would be corpses piled so high!"

"My loved ones, except Clarice, are gone. It is a cold world I enter after leaving the fortress, Louis."

"But one that you and I will share."

"Are you going with us? I thought you had to remain here."

"Someone else is taking over for me. I will be by your side all the way to the gates of the Vatican."

He smiled with such warmth that Sarah's very soul was cheered.

"And beyond," he added, "if you will let me."

"Let you? I. . .I—"

"Marry me, Sarah. If you do, with Christ's help, we can face plague and whatever else the devil throws against us."

"I am too young for you," Sarah hesitated.

"Nonsense!" he told her. "If Christ joins us together, can we expect other than a persistent joy throughout our lives? There is a reason for this today. Do not let it slip away from us, dear, dear Sarah. Do not let that happen."

"That may be a trap," she reminded him. "My mother and my father were blessed by the Lord at the very beginning of their marriage and for many years afterward, but look at what has befallen them now."

"The good years help us build up strength for the bad ones that are to come," he went on. "And the memories warm us when cold fear threatens."

"I do love you, Louis Dafoe," she whispered, slipping her arms around his neck.

His lips brushed her ear as he declared, "And we shall be married in the center of St. Peter's Square."

CHAPTER 4

Clarice was in her quarters as usual, curled up on the bed, little whimpering sounds coming from her.

As Sarah entered, Clarice glanced up and muttered a faint hello.

"Are you feeling any better?" Sarah asked.

"Numb now. The pain is gone. I cannot say that I feel anything at all."

"I have some news."

Clarice's eyes briefly opened wider.

"About Father?"

Sarah hesitated.

"That man was wrong," Clarice added before she could speak. "Tell me that this is the news you bring. If not, what is there that I should hear about anything?"

"No, it is not that, I am afraid."

Clarice turned away.

"But we have a chance now to do something that is so fine and to do it in Father's memory," Sarah told her.

"What could we do that would matter? Nothing would bring him back. What else is there? What else counts?"

"Pope Adolfo will see us. He will listen."

Clarice had been breathing heavily. Abruptly she stopped, not daring to breathe at all for a moment.

"Does that mean we can tell him what Father never had a chance to say?" she asked, hoping she had not misunderstood.

"We can do exactly that. And with Monique Dumelle's testimony, I think Baldasarre Gervasio's influence will finally be brought to an end."

Clarice sat up. Her cheeks were wet, as was the goose-down pillow where her head had rested.

"I wonder if I can face the ratman," she admitted. "I wonder if I can face him without having hidden a dagger first."

"Father would never want that."

"Are you so sure about that, Sarah? I think he would have done it himself if he had had a chance."

Sarah shook her head. "He had that chance in the catacombs."

"But did he really? He was terrorized, Sarah. He never came all that close to Gervasio. And there were always the rats."

As a child, Clarice had found the creatures to be as repugnant as her father did. She had seen scores of them in the dollhouse area of the Fothergill castle one time years before and had run screaming to her parents. As young as she had been then, the only reason she was there was to look for her cat. She had found it, and so had the rats, and the sight of what they were doing to its body robbed her of restful nights of sleep for a week after that. Servants were immediately ordered to the location and killed as many as they could find.

It did little good, she thought. *They kept multiplying. Kill a hundred, and five hundred would be found later. Kill those and—*

Clarice nodded as she said. "I just wish—"

"That Father could know what will happen soon? All of us meeting with Pope Adolfo, hopefully to settle everything."

"Yes. . . ."

"It probably no longer matters to him. He is beyond pain and fear now. The loss is not his, Clarice; it is ours, ours only."

She hoped her sister was grasping every word.

"Have you, during the past few days, thought about that? I have. Oh, I have. It has helped to keep me going."

. . .he is beyond pain and fear now.

How important it was for her to know that, to have no doubt whatever that Cyril Fothergill was at peace.

"Father's death is the greatest tragedy of our lives, but he walks with the angels now," Sarah offered. "Think of that, will you? He has seen God, Clarice. Father has been reunited with his own parents. Between him and Grandfather, there is no shame any longer, nothing but joy, pure, unlimited joy.

"Can there be any doubt that Mother is with them this very moment, dearest Clarice? I am unable to believe otherwise. How could I, as a Christian? Mother loved the Lord as much as any of us. And the sickness, whatever it was, is gone. She is healthy again. We should be rejoicing over that, you and I, rejoicing."

Sarah then tried to express something that had occurred to her the night before as she had started to fall asleep.

"They may have lived longer because we were gone," she said, venturing the notion for the first time.

Clarice's expression seemed to suggest that she thought her sister was speaking only some kind of gibberish.

"Let me explain," Sarah spoke.

"But how could you explain that?" Clarice asked disbelievingly.

"The hope of seeing us again may have given them strength, you know, may have forced them to hang on that much longer, with each new day one in which they prayed that they would see us both walk through the front door and stand before them again. They would have tried to hold on longer, hoping to see us again; they would have tried."

"But then that hope was dashed time after time after time," Clarice pointed out. "I have to believe that their will to live was squeezed from them eventually."

Sarah bowed her head.

"You are right," she said forlornly. "I was not thinking sensibly. I just wanted something to rejoice over, some little source of—"

Both were feeling the impact of what they had learned. And they hugged one another, staying like that until the tears finally passed; then the two of them sat up in bed, thinking about the next morning and what they were being called upon to do.

"So much depends upon Monique Dumelle," Clarice said. "Setting the record straight for our father rests in the hands of a prostitute."

"She was that once, but no longer."

"As far as Adolfo is concerned, she still is."

"Until he finds out about her conversion."

Sarah hugged Clarice.

"I thought we all were so safe in here, that this fortress could withstand anything," Sarah said. "Yet that woman went through such a nightmare."

Clarice grabbed her sister's hand.

"I am scared," she acknowledged. "What will we face on the road?"

"We do not go alone," Sarah reminded her, "never alone. You must remember that. These walls keep out human armies only. The rest can get through to us whether we are here or ten miles away on an unfamiliar road, out in the open."

She tapped her chest.

"Inside us," she said. "That is where the protection rests."

"Her body," Clarice recalled, "look at what they made her do to herself."

"Monique Dumelle was not a Christian then."

"I wonder if I am—"

Sarah shook her sister.

"You must never think that!" she exclaimed. "You must never allow one of the devil's greatest weapons to enslave you. Doubt is nothing more than that, you know. It might as well be a lance aimed at your heart."

The group of twenty French soldiers, two Italian monks, a

former French prostitute, and two young Englishwomen left just after sunrise the next morning.

Ahead of them was an uncertain journey of several days. Beyond that, nothing could be predicted.

"Solitary robbers will not bother us," Captain Dafoe confidently told those he was ordered to protect, "at least not during the day. At night, there is a possibility that they might try to sneak into our camp and steal whatever they can lift and take away quickly."

The three women were concerned about that, judging by their expressions.

"But you need not worry," he reassured them. "I will have two awake, on three alternating shifts, throughout the night."

And the guards were armed well with rifles and pistols, and each also had a *dague a Rouelle* of Italian origin, a form of dagger with a longer and narrower blade than other knives, useful for stabbing rather than slashing purposes. Each soldier also had a Lochabar ax, notable for its curved shape, and a bow with a quiver of arrows.

Clarice had improved a bit.

And Louis was one of the reasons.

"He is completely charming," she said as they rode in the first carriage. Brother Thaddeus, Brother Nathaniel, and Monique Dumelle were in the one just behind them. "Are you sure you want him? If not—"

Clarice found any blond-haired Frenchman to be fascinating after years of meeting the dark brown or black-haired variety, but Louis Dafoe was someone even more intriguing to her than for just that one reason.

His eyes.

They were as arresting to Clarice as they were to her sister.

I wish I had gotten to him first, she told herself.

As though sensing her thoughts, Sarah waved a finger

at her.

"Strike the thought from your mind!" she exclaimed, laughing.

Sarah was glad to see her sister smile as though she really meant it, with some color to her cheeks.

"You do seem better," she said.

"Better than yesterday? I suppose I am, Sarah. But I wonder if either of us will ever feel better in the long run."

"I think we will be what we have to be. I think we will get through whatever awaits us in Rome and on the way there, and then we will survive to the next stage in our lives, and from there we will stumble on to the one after that. We will do this because that is what our mother and our father would have wanted, and it will be done in their memory, so that we do not dishonor them in any way."

Clarice wiped her eyes after Sarah had finished.

"We will," she said. "We will do as you say, no matter how hard it is for you and for me."

CHAPTER 5

The journey was nearly half over when they encountered yet another chilling indication that, under the persistent threat of plague, everyday life throughout Europe was becoming something foreign and bizarre and, in its way, uncivilized.

"Hell has opened up and spewed forth its terrible masses," a political figure had said after returning to France from an extended stay in the Scandinavian region, where there was no evidence of an epidemic as yet.

Along the ancient route to Rome, Clarice and Sarah saw that the politician's reaction was not only accurate but prophetic.

People had approached them earlier, begging for protection, people who had become bloated, their limbs so gangrene-like in appearance that they were sickening to look at and to smell.

The odor first.

It smelled more like a sewer overflowing than anything that could be carried by a human being. The first time it was detected, Clarice became ill, and the little caravan had to stop while she relieved herself.

"What could be causing that?" Sarah asked.

Minutes before, Louis had jumped into the carriage to sit beside her, his nose testing the air.

"Corpses," he told her after a moment. "They cannot be burnt or buried quickly enough. Some are left to rot under the sun. A good breeze will carry the odor quite a distance."

"Quiet little villages once so peaceful and serene, where life could be lived with some happiness," she mused nostalgically, "now little more than mass grave sites strewn all across the continent.

"These villages were once coveted by kings and queens as hideaways to escape the pressures of ruling their countries. The more out of the way the village was, the better. I have been told that during August of each year members of the royal court headed either out to sea in their elaborate boats or to villages surrounded by mountains, where they are left alone until they have to return to their thrones again amidst all the clamor."

Gone, now, this era, though hardly an innocent one. It had been ripped from the hands of those living it, and none would ever be able to reclaim it.

There was no other answer possible, not even to the most optimistic of observers. Life would not return to normal after the epidemic subsided, whenever that might be, because "normal" no longer meant anything.

The odor. . . .

Stronger than before, closer.

And then they saw the source.

Two men and three women stood several hundred feet ahead of them, stretching out their arms as they begged for help.

"They are nearly dead, sir," one of the forward soldiers told Dafoe.

"Kill them," Louis said firmly, hiding the anguish, the gut-wrenching anguish caused by saying those words. He knew there was no alternative since they soon would be dead anyway, and the chance that they would infect others would be lessened if they were dead, no matter how awful his decision or its consequences.

"Sir?"

"Kill them, I told you."

"But, sir—"

"Yes, I know they are human beings just like us. And

they are not an opposing force ready to attack us. But the infection they carry makes them the enemy."

The other soldier nodded.

"Arrows, sir?" he asked.

"Arrows, yes, from a maximum distance. . .they make no noise."

After the other man had left, the young captain turned uneasily to Sarah, who seemed quite horrified.

"You have not, until now, seen this side of me, I know," he said.

"You gave the only order you could have given," she told him simply.

He seemed unprepared for that answer.

"The look on your face, it—"

"It shows the disgust I feel."

"But you say I have acted correctly?"

"To save us from possible contamination!" Sarah exclaimed as she reached out for him and he leaned forward slightly, her warmth reassuring. "I know, as you know, Louis, that if we do not make it to the Vatican—"

He began to cry.

"Hold me until I stop," he asked, "for I cannot let the men see me doing this. They would think me weak."

Less than a minute had passed when he pulled away, his eyes dry.

"I love you so much," he told her. "I would have ordered them to be killed if only you were involved."

"No, you would not," she told him. "You would never do that. I alone am unimportant, Louis. I could not convince Adolfo by myself. But the others, they are the necessary ones. Without them, there is no hope."

"But I could not allow you to face any kind of danger. Those poor people are riddled with the plague. Each one is like an ugly boil ready to burst open and release its poisons. I could never let you—"

"Then would we not have striven to find some other way? There is no time for that now. Look at me, my love. I tell you the truth, Louis. Look into my eyes. Do you see any lies there?"

He kissed Sarah on the forehead just once then turned toward the front of the carriage.

The arrows had been shot from their bows, hitting their targets with well-practiced accuracy, by several of the better military archers in France, a skill that the English had shown before the French mastered it as well.

Though newer to the president's military service than most of the other men in a army that tended toward grizzled veterans of faraway wars, these younger soldiers had had their share of skirmishes.

And yet none were seasoned enough to endure what would happen next.

Amidst the overwhelming sight of bloated, disease-infected bodies, the French soldiers encountered something else, vignettes that none could forget, and for a few, that meant carrying the memory with them for another half a century.

One man jammed the arrow that struck his chest farther in as he collapsed. The others, seeing this, did the same, screaming that death was not such an enemy if it came quickly rather than toyed with them by making them suffer so grievously. The response was the same for all but one of the two women, who remained standing as she screamed, "You killed my baby!" an arrow protruding from her stomach.

She tried to pull it out but could not, succeeding only in breaking it off halfway down the shaft.

"You killed my only child!" she screamed as she staggered forward.

Louis jumped off the wagon and ran toward his men.

"Back up!" he yelled. "You cannot let her get close to you. This is for your good and everyone else's."

The other soldiers started to do as he had ordered—disobeying a superior officer was one of the more serious infractions in the medieval armies of every nation—quickly putting more distance between them and the mother.

But the young man who had shot the arrow at her was immobilized and could only repeat, "Forgive me, forgive me! Please, forgive me, for—"

Louis reached, tried to grab the bow and arrow the soldier was holding.

"You have to let go!" he ordered. "She is dying anyway. Nothing can save her, whatever we might do. But if she is responsible for infecting any of us, then our own deaths are certain to come before another week is up."

The soldier was clearly close to breaking down.

"But the baby. . .I killed her baby," he said.

"The baby would have died anyway as soon as the plague claimed its mother. How could it have survived? Impossible!"

But still, the young soldier was not responding.

The woman was closer, too close.

Louis knew he had to stop her. He slipped his dagger out of its sheath and was getting ready to hurl it toward her when the soldier grabbed his wrist.

"How can you, sir?" he pleaded, desperation straining his voice. "Have I not done enough to that poor soul? Please let the woman alone."

"She is a poor soul, I agree," Louis started to say.

"Then you must do something. You cannot take her life."

"That poor soul, if she is a Christian, is far better off in heaven right now than lingering so horribly as she would for even another hour!" the young captain declared. "Do you want her to be responsible for forcing death sentences upon each of our passengers as well as ourselves?"

The soldier let go, nodding.

"Forgive me, captain, forgive me. . ." he muttered.

Louis threw the dagger, and even though his hand was

trembling the blade hit its target, entering her neck, the tip coming out the back. She died as she hit the ground. A sigh escaped lips that were riddled with blisters turned greenish with scarlet edges, her beet-red eyes remaining open, staring at the cloudless, pale blue sky.

In the evening, after camp was set up in an open field, they all shared a simple dinner of venison and cheese.

Louis had been spending most of his time with Sarah since they had left the fortress, and that did not change, but as he sat with her before one of the campfires, running his fingers through her hair, she noticed that he seemed tense and absentminded.

"Is it what happened this afternoon?" she asked without bothering to ask him if anything was wrong.

"Yes. . ." he replied. "You would think that I would have gotten over being affected by such things after my years as a soldier."

"By killing someone, you mean?"

"Killing another man whose own purpose is to do the same to me. . .that I can abide. Doing that no longer robs me of sleep. Is that not in itself an awful state to admit? I can stab my enemy through the heart and watch him fall at my feet and then, after the battle subsides, go off for some dinner and laughter with my fellow soldiers."

He stopped moving his hand, resting it on top of her head.

"My hand has been covered with blood," he sighed, "and now it rests on the soft down of an angel."

"I am not an angel," she remarked.

"You have not slept with anyone. You have not taken the life of another human being. You have never robbed anyone. Your hands are clean and pure. You are far closer to being an angel than I am."

"You have robbed someone?" Sarah asked, her body tensing a bit.

"It is called the spoils of war."

"And what about the rest of it?"

"The killings? Yes, many."

"Yes. . .have you been with other women?"

"I have, Sarah. I wish I did not have to tell you this, but I cannot add a lie to the list of my other sins."

He leaned over and pressed those wide, soft lips of his against her forehead.

"Do you hate me?" he asked earnestly. "Do you want me less?"

"I have done in thought and dream what you have done in reality."

"You have?"

"I have."

"You have stolen something?"

"To covet is to steal."

"But your family is wealthy. What could there be that you could not afford to acquire by the dozen?"

"That which I coveted could not be bought."

He became silent, waiting for her to explain what she meant.

"I coveted another woman's happiness," she continued, "looking at her with such envy as to be a stench in the presence of the Lord."

"You have been unhappy, Sarah?"

"*Unfulfilled*, I suppose, is a better word. I have seen so many women who have a healthy family of their own, some of those women hardly older than I am. I see them smile as their husbands approach them and as their children gather around, and I wonder if I am ever to be blessed in that way."

"But you are so young," Louis protested.

"To be young and yearning is a bad combination."

"But your sister is in the very same state, unmarried, and she seems to give no hint of being unsettled."

"Had you suspected this of me before I admitted it to you?"

"No, I had not."

"Then believe it to be the same with Clarice, more so since she is two years older. She must be looking at you and me, Louis, and wondering when she will be as blessed as you and I are now."

"You think us blessed?" he asked without sounding at all surprised.

"I think us so bountifully blessed that I have thanked Christ Jesus every evening since we first met."

"As I have, Sarah, as I have."

She was resting her head on his lap. He bent down and kissed her.

"You help," he told her.

"Help? With what happened today?"

"Talking about it, getting my feelings out, and yet not sounding weak. It was like I had a wound and you were the nurse who came in, saw what was wrong and now, you have treated me. I still feel the pain—I cannot tell you otherwise—but it is less now, and in time, while I may not forget it, I can live with it if you are by my side."

He seemed to want to tell her something else but was holding back.

"Is there more that you want to say?" she asked.

"Sarah. . . ?"

"Yes."

"It is difficult for me, even with you," he confessed.

"Please, Louis, tell me; tell whatever is on your heart."

"You help me to want to go on living," he said as though spitting out something from his mouth that was distasteful.

She was surprised this time.

"You do not seem like someone who would ever feel that way. You are so alive."

That was in part what had attracted her to him. She could not conceive of a dark side to this vibrant Frenchman.

"It is so hard to tell you this, so hard. . ."

His voice trailed off for a moment.

She let him be quiet for as long as he needed.

"My happiness began when we met. I came alive, truly alive the first time I held you in my arms," he finally said. "Before that happened, I could no longer look at a sunrise or a sunset and be thrilled by what I saw. I could no longer come upon a meadow filled with beautiful flowers and be touched by the sight of the blossoms or their fragrance. They meant nothing to me, these examples of God's handiwork. I was drained of joy, Sarah, drained clean of it, with thoughts of death filling my mind instead."

"But why, Louis?" she asked, alarmed that this was another side of him, one that had been hidden from her.

"Because I have brought death to so many others. Can a man live with such memories as the ones that crowd my brain?"

Louis had become quite pale.

"I warned you about the memories I have stored away," he said. "There are countless rotten images lurking here, Sarah."

"Yes, I think I understand; I really do."

"I have not told you much."

"But your mind and mine are so close now."

"You read my mind?"

"No, but it is as though I do. I can tell by the tone of your voice, by the way you set your jaw, the way your eyebrows arch at times."

He was snapping out of his melancholy.

"That reminds me, my dear Sarah."

"Reminds you of what?"

"You said a little while ago what you have done in thought and in dream. . ."

She felt ashamed, particularly after what he had just confided.

"We should not talk about this anymore," she said.

"If you are embarrassed, I understand, but I wonder if you, in your innocence, are capable of anything that would be—"

"I hope. . ."

"You hope what?"

"That we will be married soon. Could it be mere days from now? Could it really be as soon as that, Louis?"

The thought excited her but also made her nervous.

"In the middle of St. Peter's Square?"

"Yes!" she exclaimed. "And there, in the shadow of St. Peter's Basilica, I shall hold you close to me, in front of whoever is gathered near us, and regardless of what they might be thinking I will kiss you with more passion than I have ever felt before."

In a moment or two the talking ended, and they fell asleep, holding one another until dawn; then they were awakened to begin the day's journey.

CHAPTER 6

Less than a day's ride was left before they reached the outskirts of Rome.

"Our father made this same journey," Clarice was telling Louis as he sat between her and Sarah.

"It is the quickest route," he told her, "and the safest."

"Why the safest?" she asked.

"Because along this route the people rose up against the criminals who had been making their lives intolerable a few years ago. They could no longer endure being tyrannized by all the crime assaulting them—robbery, the rape of their womenfolk, vandalism—crime that robbed every man, woman, and child of the blessed tranquillity they once assumed was their God-given right, considering how close to the Vatican they are."

"Should not the Vatican have been more involved," Sarah posed an obvious question, "rather than leave these people to their own devices?"

"Of course it should have been. But the hierarchy was distracted then, and it continues to be, only to a greater extent. The Vatican is a government that finds itself in the most considerable turmoil. It is on the verge of collapse. If that happens, you will find an even worse wave of demonic influence throughout Europe."

"Because of Baldasarre Gervasio?"

"That is a good guess, and there is no question that Gervasio is at the center of what is happening. But the difficulties go beyond just one man, however fanatical he might be.

It seems that Adolfo is, however belatedly, beginning to realize this truth, from what I have been able to gather."

"You really do think so?"

"Definitely, Sarah. His blindness to the problems may not be permanent. That is what I pray, because the implications, even for those who do not accept Catholic dogma, are horrendous."

"But how is it that so many on the outside know what needs to be done, and yet the pontiff has remained so ignorant of the truth all this time?"

He held her hand in his and squeezed it gently.

"This kind of situation is something you, of all people, should understand, Sarah."

"Why? What do you mean?"

"Your entire family was unaware of the many good things your grandfather had done, the Christian side of Raymond Fothergill warring against the sinful one, spirit against flesh, flesh against spirit. For this he was rejected year after year after year. It apparently took his death to change everything."

"Yes, only then did we learn of the great number of people he had helped in those moments when the charitable side of him was in control," she acknowledged, her feeling of guilt hardly hidden. "We also came to know how much he had wanted to change and how many times Grandfather had turned to us but we would have nothing of him; the door always slammed in his face. I think it was that we were embarrassed socially by his promiscuous behavior."

"As much as by the question of his sinfulness."

"Yes," she told him, admiring his perceptiveness but hating it at the same time and becoming impatient over where he was heading.

"And all the while, not understanding that you were as guilty of sins of your own as he was of his, whether or not yours were as serious. If you could turn your back on

Raymond Fothergill, then God should be able to turn His back on you."

Sarah began to perceive the point he was making.

"Adolfo's blindness is for the opposite reason, but blindness it remains just the same," she said. "My family and I refused to acknowledge the good that was part of Grandfather's life. The pope refuses to see the evil in Gervasio's."

"You could not accept the fact that your grandfather was capable of anything kind and decent and loving. This pontiff cannot quite grasp the truth that the man he has trusted for so long is capable of the demonic acts he has committed."

"But you say he is changing."

"Some reality manages to shine through from time to time, catching his attention before Gervasio gets to it. . .first a ray here, then another there, then another, and right now, there is much going on that points to the downfall of the Catholic Church, if not right away, then a decade from now or whenever it happens, but happen it will.

"We should never allow ourselves to forget that Pope Adolfo, while terribly, terribly blind, is in the end not a stupid man at all. He seems to have started, for the first time, to restrict Gervasio's authority."

Some villagers had come out from their modest homes and were standing along the side of the road, waving at them excitedly.

"They want us to stop," Louis said.

"Should we?" Clarice asked. "We are so close. Should we not go right on ahead and not allow even the shortest delay?"

Louis hesitated.

"A few minutes," he told her. "Perhaps the road is washed out ahead or something else is wrong. It is unusual for these people to do anything but ignore a small caravan such as this."

"Wrong? You think there could be trouble?"

Clarice had come out of her depression, but she was still nervous, uncertain, ready to worry about the slightest matter.

"Look at them," he spoke.

As soon as she did, she saw what he had noticed, people who seemed terrified, who were desperate to have them stop.

"We are soldiers, after all," he reminded Clarice. "They think of us, at times like this, as protectors."

Louis jumped off his horse and went from man to woman to man, talking with each one, trying to get an idea of what they wanted. He shook hands with them and then got back into the carriage.

"They are afraid," he said.

"Why?" Clarice asked.

"The flagellants."

"We have seen none of their kind."

"Ahead. The flagellants are going from village to village, home to home, not caring how they hurt any people who might happen to be in their way."

"For what reason?"

"Jews."

"They are after some Jews?"

"*All* Jews," he told her. "They are blaming the Jews for the plague and whatever other charge they can concoct."

"So close to the Vatican!" Sarah exclaimed.

"A rumor has started," Louis told them both.

"What sort of rumor?" Clarice asked.

"About Adolfo."

"Has something happened to him?"

"No. The pontiff has assembled a significant force that is comprised of his finest soldiers, the veteran elite members of the Vatican Guards. And he is personally going to lead it in action against the flagellants if they resist his commands."

Both sisters were starting to feel excited.

"Adolfo is taking action at last!" Sarah blurted out with gusto. "Praise God, Louis! Praise God above!"

"There is a problem," he said slowly, not wanting to alarm them, but at the same time he was reluctant to withhold anything.

"Tell us," Sarah said. "Please tell us, Louis."

"Just up ahead, the flagellants are herding some Jews into a barn."

"Why would they want to do that?"

"To torture them or—"

"Burn it down, killing them all!" Sarah exclaimed. "I heard that that had happened in a hamlet in Switzerland, not far from where Clarice and I had been staying; two hundred men, women, and children were locked inside a bar, and the flagellants burned it to the ground."

"Will Adolfo get there in time?"

"I doubt it. He is at least an hour's ride from here. But we are just minutes away."

"Can we do anything to help?"

"We may be able to, Sarah. I know we must try. Three of the men from the village here want to join us. They are tired of being terrorized."

"Will you let them?"

It was Clarice this time.

"They have pitchforks with them."

"Where?"

"In the ditch beside the road."

"I told those men they should follow along behind us and they are free to help, but only if it is necessary. However, the women will have to stay behind. There should be no argument about this. I insisted that was my only condition."

Louis put one arm around Clarice, the second around Sarah, and they bowed their heads in prayer, then he jumped off the carriage and onto the back of his horse, going from soldier to soldier and instructing each one.

Clarice moved next to her sister.

"I am afraid," she said. "I am very afraid."

"Do we have a choice?" Sarah asked.

Clarice shook her head.

"We do not; that is what makes me feel so helpless. If we could just turn around and enter Rome another way. If we could just recognize that—"

She stopped herself.

"I know, Sarah. This fight may not be ours but what do we have to lose, fighting it? If Father and Mother are able to see us now, how proud they would be of us if we became a part of it. And how ashamed if we turned and ran!"

"Pope Adolfo is apparently headed this way with his Vatican Guards. The Lord might be bringing him to us rather than the other way around. Is that not something? We might have to do little to convince him."

"I love you," Clarice said as she put her arms around her sister. "We have no one else now. We live together; we die together. That is the way it is for you, and for me."

CHAPTER 7

Two hundred Jews, their ragged clothes in a pile to one side. . . .

"We make an example of these creatures practically in the shadow of the Vatican," the flagellant leader, a bald-headed, broad-shouldered, overweight bull of a man named Guiseppe Zangari, roared from his horse as the line of frightened adults and children were directed toward the barn. "Adolfo will have to listen to us now and stop turning his back on decent people in favor of scum."

The Jews chosen by Zangari ran a spectrum of ages and types. Some of the Jewish men were so old they had to be helped along by others far younger. Two of the women were pregnant. The children looked as if they ranged in age from three or four up to fifteen, sixteen, and seventeen.

But it was the pregnant women who delighted him most.

"Two in one!" Zangari joked. "What a wonderful bonus! This generation and a future one."

One of the women stopped briefly and glowered at him.

"What is it that you want?" he asked, assuming a much more paternalistic tone.

"Why are you doing this to us?" she demanded.

"To get you clean."

"Clean for what?"

"Some new work."

"My family and I are not poor. We do not need any such work."

"Yes, you do."

"Only because you and your henchmen took everything we have. Your saddlebags bulge with our wealth."

"I am simply holding it for you. These are hard times. You should never keep your valuables at home. Robbers can grab them from you."

"But you and your wicked men are worse than robbers. You claim God's will as you commit your thievery and all the rest. That is blasphemy!"

Zangari slid off his horse and waddled up to the woman. She was the last Jew outside by then. All the others were in the barn.

"Who are you to talk of blasphemy?" he shouted.

"And what are you? A walrus who can get attention only when he torments pregnant women and beats up old men."

She pointed her finger at him.

"I saw you back in Switzerland, the atrocities you engaged in there. I was fortunate enough. I escaped, but two hundred others did not. They—"

Her mouth dropped open in shock.

"You are going to do the same thing here!" she exclaimed, suddenly linking the two events. "You—"

The woman did not finish because he took a dagger and stabbed her in the chest just once. She crumpled in an instant at his feet. Zangari spat on her forehead and remounted his horse.

Leonardo Ragusi, the gray-haired, middle-aged flagellant on the horse next to him, was not pleased. He was a holdover from the old school, the one supporting the idea that the road to heaven could be better traveled by inflicting pain on one's own body but not on others, for that was cruel, something more akin to the Roman Empire than to Christian Europe. Even so, he had sacrificed whatever values he had clung to by instead staying on, by becoming Zangari's lieutenant, as it were. If he had bolted earlier, he would have been tracked down and killed, an inch at a time.

Zangari added, "The Jewish masses are like cattle. You know, it is disappointingly easy to get them to obey any command."

"They have been that way for centuries," Ragusi replied.

"What way?" Zangari asked.

"Like lemmings rushing to their own slaughter."

Zangari sneered, the image a comfortable one that reinforced his anti-Semitic philosophy, which he was now able to inflict on those who were its object.

"Cowards then, of course. Not surprising!"

Ragusi shook his head.

"I think it is something else. They are convinced that they all will be wiped out someday, so why make things worse by resisting?"

"You should be appointed the wise man of our group," bellowed Zangari, not without some sincerity.

"I need no such appointment, Guiseppe. I already am the wise man."

Zangari laughed heartily at that example of sardonic humor and refocused his attention on the still-open barn doors.

A moment later he told the other man, "Get everything ready, Leonardo. I give my speech to them now."

"The standard one?"

"Only that. Do they deserve more?"

"Of course not."

Zangari rode up to the open doorway and squinted as he peered inside, the odors of sweat and urine already prominent.

"You are to be our slaves," he told them, disgusted. "But you must be clean first. We do not want to see or smell your filthy hides any longer."

"We cannot find the soap," someone called out from inside the barn. "It is so dark in here. Where is the water— and our new clothes that you promised?"

"I know the water is here. Wait a few minutes. I will

make sure you get your soap. After that, we will wait fifteen minutes. All of you had better be cleaned and dressed by the time we open those doors again."

And then the doors were slammed shut and locked by a flagellant on each side.

"Has the dry brush been placed around the entire building?" Zangari asked.

"As always, sir," one of the men replied.

"Do it again. Another layer. I want to take precautions. None must escape."

The young man, still in his teens, bowed obediently and hurried off.

Zangari rode his horse a safe distance from the old barn, but not so far that he could not hear the Jews scream.

Louis asked the villagers to stand guard around Clarice and Sarah as well as around Brother Thaddeus and Brother Nathaniel.

The villagers agreed. One of them said something that was no longer as surprising as it once had been.

"Fothergill?" the robust young man named Camillo repeated. "Are you related to Raymond Fothergill?"

Clarice answered for both of them.

"We are his granddaughters," she said.

At that the four villagers fell to their knees and crossed themselves.

"What is wrong with you?" Louis asked, wondering with whom he was leaving the safety of his four charges.

They stood, and Camillo spoke up enthusiastically, "Raymond Fothergill did many wonderful things for our village. We were starving in the midst of the famine, and he rented a very big boat that brought in goods from northern Africa and the Arabs."

"The Arabs allowed this to happen?" Louis asked, not prepared to ask that at face value. "They would have preferred you dead!"

"It was because of Raymond Fothergill. He had a way of talking anyone into anything," Camillo retorted but not unpleasantly.

Again both sisters were learning more about their grandfather's activities but wished they had known of it sooner.

"What a difference it could have made if we had learned this before!" Clarice exclaimed.

Camillo heard this and smiled disarmingly, his rugged but handsome face not going unnoticed by Clarice.

"He did it in love," the villager said. "May I speak freely? Even by doing so I may cause some offense."

She told him he could.

"He gave that love to all of us because you would not accept it from him."

Clarice stiffened, and Louis started to walk toward the villager, but she raised her hand, and he stopped.

"We never knew," she said sadly. "We—"

"Thank God we now have a chance to do something for his loved ones," Camillo told her. "My wife and two boys would be dead today if it were not for that man. I could never turn my back on you."

The other men from the village expressed their agreement with that.

"We must go," Louis said warily. "Before long, the flagellants will have—"

Smoke.

Almost on cue, the odor of smoke started from rotten old wood drifted past, confirming his judgment.

"Already!" Louis yelled as he turned to the other soldiers. "We have to hurry! On your horses. . .we ride now."

He turned and led his men in a charge across the wide, old road and onto the farm acreage where the barn imprisoning the two hundred Jews stood, fire already beginning.

The flagellants were gathered about a hundred feet from

the barn, thirty-five of them sitting on the soft grass and watching one side of the barn ignite, then another side. They were laughing boisterously.

Louis sent two of his men toward the building either to stamp out the fire or, more likely, to break down one of the doors so that those trapped inside could be released. The others stayed behind, just out of sight.

Alone, Louis rode in front of the flagellants, who were startled by the intrusion.

"You are ordered to disband!" Louis demanded.

Guiseppe Zangari stood.

"And who is giving the order?" he spoke sarcastically.

"Captain Louis Dafoe of—"

"The French Army, I see."

"Yes, under order of—"

"You have no jurisdiction here."

Louis smiled broadly as he retrieved a crumpled scroll from an inside pocket of his uniform.

"Pope Adolfo anticipated something like this," he said. "I have here a proclamation signed by the holy father himself."

"Nonsense," Zangari grumbled, aware that his credibility was at stake with the flagellants. "Let me examine that."

Zangari walked up to Louis's horse and held out his hand. Louis bent down and turned the scroll over to him.

Zangari skimmed the contents then tore it into several small pieces and let a stiff breeze scatter it in every direction.

"I see no proclamation!" he exclaimed, turning to the others and asking for their response.

As one they roared back, "Neither do we!"

"Wrong!" Louis retorted exuberantly.

Another copy appeared, this one taken from one of his saddlebags.

"Would you like to read it again?" he asked with pseudo-politeness.

Zangari hesitated then placed his hands on his hips.

"I think whatever you have is a forgery," he said. "I cannot obey whatever I suspect to be fraudulent, now, can I?"

"I suggest that you get out of the way," someone shouted from the group now standing behind Zangari. "You are interrupting our show."

"My men are even now releasing those poor, would-be victims of yours and the other madmen who have chosen to follow as you march toward your master in hell!" Louis fired back at him.

"Are you so sure, Captain?" Zangari answered. "Look behind you."

Louis turned his head and felt a wave of nausea.

Both of the men he had sent to rescue the Jews had been captured and tied to makeshift crosses.

"I was prepared for someone's moral indignation," Zangari said. "I just did not know it would be yours. We had been thinking of bringing justice to all this 'cleansing' by crucifying two Jews for a change. But your men will do for the time being."

His eyes narrowed.

"You had better leave, Captain," he said. "You have no other choice! I will release those two fools as soon as you have disappeared from sight."

Louis was sweating. He did not believe Zangari, but his men had not yet been torched. He knew he could not reach them without being attacked.

So he started to ride off then stopped suddenly and turned the horse around to allow him to face the flagellants.

"Release my men!" he shouted.

Zangari turned and gave the order to torch the two French soldiers.

Louis raised his arm, then dropped it.

A wave of arrows pierced the air in that first wave, then another wave followed seconds later. The aim of the hidden

French archers was uncanny. One flagellant after the other was hit.

But several escaped the attack, rushing toward Louis. As they approached him, they drew their swords. His horse bolted, and he fell.

Three other flagellants hurried toward the soldiers strung up on crosses but were felled by more arrows.

Yet Guiseppe Zangari stood in the middle of the chaos, defying the archers.

"You have hit the others," he shouted, "but you can never strike me down. Almighty God Most High protects my righteous cause! Everyone else is expendable except me. I shall prevail!"

The flagellants advancing on Louis stopped.

. . .*everyone else is expendable.*

Louis shuddered as Zangari spoke the name of divinity, and watched Zangari's men die in seconds as three arrows hit one and five found their mark in the other, two in his chest, one in his neck, and the last in his stomach.

"The leader!" Louis yelled at the archers who had now stepped out the row of trees behind which they had been hiding.

They aimed at Zangari.

More than a dozen arrows missed him, but one did lodge in Zangari's left shoulder. He stopped, pulled it out, contemptuously broke it in half, and continued toward the men on the crosses.

"He feels no pain!" one of the archers gasped. "How could he not feel—?"

"The man thrives on it," Louis interrupted. "Remember, he is a flagellant. Stop! Concentrate on the others. I'll go after this devil."

Zangari made it to the two crude wooden crosses before Louis could catch up with him. He spat in the faces of the two French soldiers, lifted a torch from a nearby pitchpot, and lit it from the flames now spewing out of the barn.

"May the games never end!" he yelled and held the torch up to one cross then the other.

"No!" Louis called out desperately, only a few feet away by then. "You will not commit this ungodly—!"

Zangari answered, "I already have, fool!" as Louis hit him full force and the two sprawled on the ground.

The flagellant's weight proved an asset at first, added to his unexpected strength. As he stood, he had his hands around the young captain's neck, lifting him from the ground.

"Suffocation is a delicious way to die," he growled. "The pain is just unbearable, Captain. Imagine that!"

Louis beat at Zangari's bloated face. The flagellant staggered yet kept his grip tight. But he could not be careful where he stepped. He backed up against the red-hot outer wall of the barn, and his clothes caught fire.

But still Zangari's grip was unrelenting.

"I love it!" he cried. "I crave the pain. Pain is my narcotic, can you not understand that? To die in pain is but my God's greatest blessing."

The sheer blasphemy of that claim stirred Louis, who hit Zangari with his own forehead, once, again, and yet a third time. The flagellant finally let go, and Louis dropped to the ground, flames working their way down his body.

Louis managed to get to his feet and staggered toward the two crosses.

His men were nearly consumed by fire.

"No. . . ." one of them cried. "Leave us. . .we are gone already. . .help those poor souls inside the barn. . .you might be able to save a few."

Louis looked at the other man who was nodding.

"God Himself has your reward. . .my comrades," he said, his voice breaking as tears started down his cheeks.

"We. . .see. . .the. . .blessed. . .angels. . .already. . .my captain. . .my friend."

Louis turned and waved for the archers but need not have, for they were already running toward him, as were the rest of the soldiers.

Less than a second later, the barn wall behind him collapsed inward, and he saw the holocaust inside, men and women and children running in terror to avoid falling timbers and other pieces of blazing wood, most of them catching fire before his eyes and screaming.

A mother and her little baby.

She was standing in the middle of the barn, shouting pitiably, "Help me! I care not about myself. But my baby here!"

The woman was hardly able to stand, her eyelids half-closed as she fought sudden weakness.

"Please. . .will someone take him? . . . Please do not let him die before he has been able to live!"

Louis took off the upper part of his uniform and, holding it over his back and head, rushed inside.

"God sent you!" she cried.

"Follow me!" he said, taking her hand.

"No. . .I will not make it. I am too weak."

"I will carry you then."

"You cannot," she begged. "Take my baby, and leave me behind."

"I will take him, but you must come, too."

She shook her head and stepped back into the flames directly behind her, hands pressed together in prayer.

The way he had come was now blocked by a wall of fire and fallen bodies.

Only the thicker front door ahead of him was intact. He had to get to it and push it open.

People were becoming blackened husks all around him.

The baby was crying fearfully.

"I hope to be a father to a child like you someday," he whispered hoarsely. "My beloved will carry my child as your mother carried you. Be calm, dear one. If God wills, I shall get you through this."

"Yea, though I walk through the valley of the shadow of death. . ." he repeated, and then he added, "Let me survive, dear Lord, to be with my beloved again."

Trying not to inhale the thickening smoke, Louis jumped over the sprawled bodies and through the flames, making it to the front door of the barn.

A groaning sound, not from a dying man or woman. Above.

The roof was ready to fall, and it was protesting.

Louis tried the front door, heavy under normal conditions, built of wood that had lasted through centuries.

It would not move.

Louis could not rest the baby on the floor. All around his feet were the remains of the timbers that had supported the roof, now become blazing hot coals of wood.

Once more, Lord, he prayed, *if not for me, then this littlest of Your creations.*

French Army Captain Louis Dafoe pulled the door open as the entire roof of that ancient barn gave way.

Clarice and Sarah could see the smoke.

"We can wait no longer," Clarice told one of the villagers. "We have to see what is happening. We have to know."

"Louis!" Sarah added. "I must find out what—"

She had spoken in a particularly impassioned manner, so much so that everyone was looking at her.

But she did not care what they might be thinking. She dashed across the road, followed by her sister and, belatedly, the villagers as well.

Flagellant bodies were piled in one section. The French archers were in another corner, their bows and clusters of arrows on the ground, their hats in their hands, heads bowed.

"Captain Dafoe!" Sarah asked. "Where is he?"

One of the men pointed toward the barn, which had started to collapse.

"In there?" Sarah asked hysterically.

The young soldier nodded sadly.

Sarah sank to her knees, sobbing.

Then she heard the men shouting behind her and glanced up. At first she could not see clearly, then she noticed a figure stumbling through the now open front door of the barn, a tiny baby in his arms. But his features were barely distinguishable because his long blond hair was on fire. He could have dropped the child and tried to put out the flames, but he chose instead to get the baby as far away as possible from the burning building.

"Louis!" Sarah screamed as she started to rush toward him.

At first no one saw the partially burnt, hulking figure stand uncertainly, then with more confidence, and lurch toward the French captain, sunlight striking the long, flat blade of a raised dagger.

Except Clarice.

Seeing her sister racing toward Louis, Clarice screamed at the archers, pointing toward the other man.

They quickly picked up their weapons and were ready to hit that figure with a dozen or more arrows, but by then he was too close. Some arrows might strike their captain or Sarah or both.

Clarice used whatever energy she possessed to sprint ahead, and she approached Guiseppe Zangari seconds before he would have been upon Louis or her sister, slashing at them.

She jumped on his back and managed to knock him off balance. He staggered and fell, the dagger still in his hand. Clarice was on top of him, hitting him with her fists, making him cry out in agony as she pounded the burnt flesh of his neck and shoulders.

Louis had reached Sarah and was handing her the baby.

"Clarice!" she said. "Clarice! He will kill her, Louis, he will—"

The young Frenchman's face was barely recognizable, the hair gone, the lips—"I. . .love. . .you. . .never. . .doubt. . . that," he managed to say.

"I never shall, my beloved. God knows I never shall," Sarah whispered.

And then he lurched toward Zangari, pulling him away from Clarice. The flagellant easily broke Louis's hold on his neck and flung him to one side.

Zangari stood, the blade of his dagger dripping with blood, Clarice Fothergill's blood.

"I am Guiseppe Zangari," he proclaimed, "messenger of the Most High God!"

Despite his bulk he managed to evade most of the arrows, though three hit their target. One by one, Zangari pulled them out, breaking each in half and tossing them to one side.

Clarice had been stabbed in the shoulder. She tried to crawl away, moaning as pain raced through her body.

Zangari looked down at her, sneering, and tightened his grip on the dagger as he fell across her, jabbing her again and again.

Sarah rested the baby gently on the grass and raced toward him.

"No!" she heard someone shout.

It was Louis. He had gotten to his feet and had nearly reached Zangari again. But once more this forced the archers to stop. And no one else was close enough to help.

Louis jumped Zangari, knocking the dagger out of his hand and tumbling the much larger Italian to one side, but then the young captain's strength gave out, and he fell back against the ground.

Zangari spotted the dagger and crawled toward it, knowing that if he stood again, the archers would have him, and he was now too weak to withstand their barrage. His fingers were inches from the weapon, but Sarah got to it before he did.

"Can you, innocent child that you are, kill an unarmed man?" he said as he suddenly coughed up some blood.

"I am not a child any longer," she retorted, "and as of this moment, my innocence is gone."

"Where is Gervasio when I need him?" he gasped.

At the sound of that name, Sarah plunged the dagger into Zangari's chest—just once, because the resulting blood flow and the groan he uttered made her back away in sudden shock. One last breath escaped that grotesque body of his, and after that, nothing more came from him, eyes frozen open, a thin line of spittle dribbling from between his lips.

Sarah stood and hurried to her sister's side.

At first it seemed to her that Clarice was still breathing, but Sarah saw that this was only a breeze touching the upper part of her shirt, giving an imitation of life but nothing more than that.

Clarice was gone.

A look of pain had been etched across her face, the lips twisted as though, in dying, she had started to scream.

Sarah herself was nearly unconscious, and she fell across her sister's chest.

"I have lost you, I have lost—" she cried out.

"Sarah. . ."

Louis was calling to her.

As she turned to hurry the short distance to his side, she saw the archers drop their weapons and bow their heads reverentially.

Bless you, she thought.

She sat beside Louis and reached out for his hand, but it had been burnt too badly, and he could not bear for her to touch it.

"My dearest," she said softly. "Oh, God, help him! He must not die. He must not—"

Louis's face had started to swell already, fluids trapped between layers of tortured flesh.

"I cannot even kiss you," she whispered. "I cannot hold you. I—"

His eyes were open, and he was trying to talk, but she could not hear what he was saying. She bent down, her ear next to his mouth.

"Let. . .me. . .go. . .my sweet, sweet angel!" he pleaded.

"The Lord will pull you through," she told him. "He will not allow—"

"Let. . .me. . .go. . .to. . .be. . .with. . .Him," he spoke, as though not hearing what she had said. "The pain. . .Sarah. . . you cannot know how bad the pain is!"

"But how can I lose you? How—?"

She was startled as hands fell upon her shoulders so gently that they seemed like feathers touching her.

She turned and saw a man in a long, white robe smiling at her.

"You must let him go," the stranger told her gently. "There is nothing here for him anymore. The moment his soul leaves that body you see, he will be free; he will know only peace and the purest joy for eternity. If you love him, you must not ask him to linger as he is."

"I have no one," she cried. "I have no one left. You must see that. You must know why I have to stay here at his side."

"You have God's people. We shall gather around you now. Believe that; believe it with every bit of faith and trust that you can."

Sarah Fothergill collapsed in his arms, and Pope Adolfo carried her to his waiting papal carriage in which she would be taken to the Vatican and ministered to diligently by the finest doctors in the land.

She could not hear Captain Louis Dafoe of the French army whisper his last good-bye as a single tear trickled down his burnt, blistered cheek, just before his men gathered around him, and cried their own.

CHAPTER 8

Sarah regained consciousness but against her will. She tried to cling to the darkness as though it were something physical, something that would never leave her if only she did not let go. Better the darkness than what light would bring.

Pope Adolfo was sitting at the side of the bed in which she found herself, a trio of Vatican physicians standing anxiously at the foot.

Sarah wanted to cry, to demand that she be returned to nothingness, but he would have none of that.

"You feel as you do now," he said, "but tomorrow it will be a little less, and the day after that, less still. You will hold onto life, though, because there is much ahead for you. Anything else would displease the Heavenly Father."

She did not feel respectful toward any human authority, because none that were human had helped her avoid tragedy and because it could be argued that this particular authority was at the center of what had torn her life apart, if not by commission, then clearly through blind omission.

"Much ahead for me?" she protested. "Because of you, I have nothing. Forgive me for not addressing you as holy father or any of those other titles. You are not, to me, a symbol of anything that is holy."

The three physicians mumbled to one another about the young woman's insolence.

Adolfo waved them to silence.

"When I lost those I loved, I reacted as you do now," he told her. "I will pay no attention; I will hold nothing against you, whatever you might say in your anger and your mourning. Nor will the Heavenly Father."

"But *you* are responsible!" Sarah persisted.

Adolfo indicated that the three men should immediately leave the room, and they did so without hesitation, casting pitying glances at her as they walked past and the last one quietly shut the door behind him.

"I must tell you that the fact you have been blessed with a father such as Cyril Fothergill is what cautions me against taking any action—" he started to say.

Sarah interrupted him.

"Taking any action?" she repeated angrily. "When has that been one of your virtues?"

She sat up in bed.

"As for being blessed with a father such as I have had, he was, after all, the man you tried to hunt down for crimes he never committed!"

Adolfo winced at that and pondered how he should respond. A pontiff accustomed to the unbroken attention of all who were in his presence and servitude from not a few, he tried to speak but was shouted down by a twenty-year-old woman just emerged from unconsciousness. And he could do nothing but listen.

"You chose to believe Baldasarre Gervasio instead of a man like Cyril Fothergill!" she declared. "And look what happened! If you had believed my father, millions of people would be alive today. I have no idea who most of them are. But I do know of my father, and I know—"

She hesitated, trying not to cry, trying to be firm and strong.

"—of Captain Louis Dafoe."

Despite her intentions, she had to pause again as she thought of those last grisly moments, of that once handsome face turned into something so repulsive that she needed to force herself not to turn away in disgust.

"When I saw Louis like that," Sarah recalled out loud, "when I heard him moaning from unspeakable pain, I wanted to—"

She covered her mouth with her left hand.

"It is so hard," she continued. "You cannot know how hard it is for me! I *wanted* my beloved to die. I *wanted* my dashing young captain to die! How could I want that? How could I give him up? How could I not want him to survive, whatever his appearance, because, if he lived I could still hold him, still pretend he was the same inside?

"Do you not understand what I am saying? But instead I prayed, 'Lord, take him. He will suffer the rest of his life even if he is strong enough to go on. I could not endure that, Lord. Please take him into Your kingdom and let him—' "

"Young woman. . ." Adolfo said, seeing that she was working herself into a fresh bout of hysteria.

"No!" Sarah cried out. "I am not finished. I do not know when I shall ever be finished."

"You only do injury to yourself," he pleaded, earnestly concerned for her welfare.

"Should I care any longer about what happens to me? Is there someone to whom I can go for solace? I know how those millions of victims' loved ones feel. Oh, how I know! If all those now dead left loved ones behind, I feel as those survivors feel, and I ache as they ache."

Adolfo reached out a hand to touch her on the shoulder, but she turned away from him, slid down, and buried her face in an extraordinarily soft pillow.

"Everyone is gone!" she sobbed. "Those I have known and loved since birth, and the man with whom I would have spent the rest of my life."

For the next half hour, Adolfo let her calm down until the sobs were ceasing, her body no longer convulsing.

"May I speak now?" he asked.

Sarah said nothing in response.

"Believe what I say," he began. "Believe me when I tell you that I know I am responsible for twelve million people dead so far and many more expected to follow. That is what you have been saying, and you are right."

. . .twelve million people dead so far.

Sarah had not dared to think of such a number. She wondered if her father had heard anything of it and would not have been surprised if it had been the second reason for his death, apart from seeing Elizabeth taken from him ounce by ounce, pound by pound, becoming even thinner than she was when they left.

"How can you ever wash their blood off your hands?" she asked, sitting up in bed again and staring at the pontiff.

"I have no hope of doing so, Sarah Fothergill," he acknowledged. "I shall carry the knowledge with me until that much-craved day when I am called to the gates of the heavenly kingdom and unless, Almighty God has changed His mind in my regard, I shall be allowed past. I will look for your father, Sarah, and I shall tell him of my shame and my regret."

"But it is my mother as well," she told him. "Father's death must have inflicted upon her a burden so intolerable that, even if she were well, she could not have borne it. Her death could only have been hastened."

He stood and paced the floor of that room deep within St. Peter's Basilica, a room filled with choice, imported furniture and elaborate tapestries. Above them was a ceiling on which was displayed an artist's rendering of the resurrection of Christ.

"I can offer only one matter over which you might want to rejoice," he said. "Two days ago, Baldasarre Gervasio was imprisoned in a dungeon not more than a hundred yards from where he raised his rats."

"You learned the truth about him?" she asked, straightening up even more.

"I did, but I am afraid I was too late by a number of years."

Sarah wanted to hate this man whom so many came perilously close to worshiping, but now he seemed, if anything, as vulnerable as she was.

"Your physicians are waiting," she reminded him. "Should you not be leaving now?"

"It is you who are important, Sarah," Adolfo said. "They can wait."

"You have lost also. . ." Sarah observed, examining his face. "I see this in your eyes."

"How could one so young know such things?"

"I think the past six months have aged all of us."

"Not as greatly as you, but yes, I have been alone in my study or my bedroom, and there have been tears. My half brother Maximillian, for one, Sarah."

"Captain Letchworth!"

"Yes! You knew him."

"My father did. He was with your brother on that last voyage."

They continued talking for many more hours, confounding those members of the papal staff who waited in the hallway outside. Only servants with food at lunchtime and at dinner were allowed into the bedroom.

CHAPTER 9

That time spent between just the two of them changed them both. For Sarah, it involved a sudden, concentrated series of steps that pulled her back from the brink of death. For Adolfo, it was the final pulling aside of a curtain that had been draped between him and the rest of the world. In the past, whenever he had reached out toward it, Baldasarre Gervasio, however artfully, had pulled it out of his hand, and it would drop back into place.

"I have been guilty of blind faith, yes," he acknowledged. "And like someone in that state, I depended upon people around me, as though I had no sight of my own. Blind faith in the Savior is not in error; it never could be. But it cannot be placed in mere mortal people. They remain creatures of sin, as I am."

"What was there about Gervasio that fooled you?" Sarah asked.

"I think he knew how to translate pity into obligation."

He saw that she was frowning, so he elaborated.

"When you are in London and you see a beggar," Adolfo asked, "what is your reaction? Do you cross the street to avoid him?"

"No," Sarah said, "I give him a coin if I have any with me. Father taught us if we had no money on our person, then we should take the beggar into a bakery or an eatery where he could get something to fill his stomach. Failing that, we should become a beggar as well by going to someone we know, and asking money of him or her."

"Have you ever passed by a beggar?"

Adolfo knew that Sarah would be truthful, and he was eager to learn what that truth was.

She thought carefully for a moment.

"No, I am not able to remember any," she replied, satisfied that she was not hiding anything from him.

Adolfo seemed certain that, as intelligent as she was, Sarah would see what his point was without further commentary on his part.

"Then you know, once you think about it, how Baldasarre Gervasio worked himself into the position he had, and you understand the power it brought to him. And now you can understand what I meant when I spoke of pity being translated into obligation."

"What about Monique Dumelle?" Sarah asked.

Adolfo had been wiping his lips with a silk napkin.

"I saw that she was one of those in your group," he recalled, trying to appear matter-of-fact in his response.

"I met her in the fortress."

"She is a witch, you know. I hesitated bringing her inside St. Peter's. Others who know about her might be worried about her influence. But under the circumstances, I could not find suitable justification for barring her."

"She *was* a witch," Sarah corrected him.

Adolfo's eyebrows arched.

"But I know what she has done, the rites, the—"

"No longer," she interrupted.

She smiled as she told him what had happened.

"Monique has converted to Christ."

He dropped the napkin on the ground and leaned forward, placing his hands over his face and weeping.

Sarah got out of bed and walked over to him.

"What have I said?" she asked, concerned.

"I am not distressed," he said, taking his hands away and dropping them at his side. "I am very happy."

"Would you tell me why?" she asked, not persuaded.

"I thought Monique Dumelle might have been innocent of charges of treason. My instincts told me she was. But Gervasio seemed so certain. What was I to do? Accept the word of a witch who also was a common prostitute? Or the word of the most important member of my staff?"

She could see the depth of his frustration.

"That woman tried so very hard to convince me that she was not the traitor Gervasio pictured her to be."

"If you knew about her being what she was, not a traitor, I mean, but the rest, were you not anxious to know why Gervasio allowed her to get so close to him in the first place?"

Adolfo's cheeks were becoming tinged with red.

"I knew none of it," he admitted.

"Nothing?"

"He told me she was someone he was counseling, not sleeping with."

"You did not question him to find out if he was hiding anything?"

"If I had believed an affair between them to have been possible, I would have done something about it without fail. When Gervasio turned on that woman without any seeming compunction, he did it with a most pathetic edge, painting himself as the one who was deceived, not the deceiver. I had to accept his word."

Adolfo sounded frustrated.

"Was I to cast him out, and not Monique Dumelle?" he asked reasonably. "Could I be expected to do so?"

Adolfo stood and began pacing once again.

"I come to you seeming like a fool, do I not?" he spoke.

"Not long ago," Sarah confessed, "I would have called you worse."

He stopped and looked up at the majestically high ceiling.

"But am I so alone in being duped as I have been?" he

pleaded. "Was not Caesar betrayed by those he had trusted far longer than I have known Gervasio?"

Suddenly his body stiffened, and color drained from his face.

"Father God!" he exclaimed. "Could it be—?"

He seemed to become faint and leaned against the bed-post for support.

"Can I help?" Sarah asked. "Do you want anyone from outside to—?"

Adolfo waved his hand through the air.

"They would but give me the wrong answer, the pleasing one, the flattering, reassuring answer to what I have just real-ized. And they would do this because they have become accustomed to it. If I learn of bad news, they remind me of the good, or they make the bad seem not so awful after all. It is their job, you know, the maintenance of my physical and my mental well-being because, it is assumed, with these aspects of my life looked after, I would not be troubled spiritually."

"You are so pale," she said.

Adolfo sat down, and Sarah joined him.

"I think you may have been right," he said.

"Right about what?"

"Whenever you happened, in those days before this one, to have called me worse than a fool."

"I suspect now that I was very wrong."

"But what were you thinking? That I was weak in addi-tion to being foolish?"

"Worse."

"Please tell me, good Sarah."

Seeing Adolfo for what he was, she was uncomfortable telling the pontiff what she once had thought him to be.

"I will not be angry," he promised.

Still, she was reluctant.

"From now on I want only to embrace the truth, shorn of Baldasarre Gervasio's deceptions. Will you help me begin by telling me now what you once considered me to be?"

"Can you be so sure you want to know?"

"I am not, as you say, so sure I want to know," he said, "but I am convinced that I must know."

He was close to begging her.

"You will tell me, please," Adolfo asked again.

"I thought—and my father came to believe this as well —I thought you were serving Satan, not God, that you might have been a demon posing as an angel of light."

Adolfo groaned as she spoke.

. . .*a demon posing as an angel of light.*

"Was that what you also thought of a moment ago," Sarah asked, "when you reacted so sharply?"

"No. It was something else, different and yet much the same."

She was looking puzzled again.

"Am I talking in riddles?"

"You are."

Adolfo inhaled, giving the impression of a man who was confronting one of the more difficult tasks of his life.

"I shall try to explain. . ." he sighed.

He pressed his hands together and brought them to his lips as he concentrated on expressing himself.

"Only Christ as a man was infallible, is that not what you believe?" he asked.

"I do."

"Secretly, in the dark hallways of my soul, which I tried never to enter but found myself there anyway, secretly I felt that I was infallible also."

Sarah had not suspected anything as extreme as that.

"Infallible like Christ?"

"Yes!" he exclaimed. "The original popes were not like that, you know. They sacrificed wealth; they did not hoard it. They would have been repulsed by the wanton display of all that you see here.

"But as the religion changed from one of Christlike simplicity to what it is now, so the grandeur of their opinions of themselves and their stations became exaggerated, distorted beyond anything that was holy."

Suddenly Adolfo fell backward, hitting the bed and lying there motionlessly.

"I will call for someone to come in," she said.

As she was getting up, he reached out and grabbed her hand.

"You must not," Adolfo begged her. "You must let me pass through this exorcism, and it is that, in a way. If not an exorcism of actual demons, then it is an exorcism of a corruption of the conscience that is well-nigh as bad, for it can only be a product of demonic design. You must help me drain the pus from this wound of the spirit, the soul.

"I may have only this one chance to do that, to do it with just you here, for you will soon be returning to your native England, but the others will stay on until that moment when I shall die. And facing them daily, suspecting what is being said behind my back, is not how I wish to spend the rest of my life."

"Why? What do you mean?"

"They would use this against me."

"What?" Sarah said, raising her voice.

He wiped his eyes and sat up.

"Oh, that is what it is like behind these massive walls," he told her. "You cannot conceive of the intrigue."

Intrigue at the center of the established church. . . .

Adolfo was right. She would not have been able to picture such a thing before this moment.

"Gervasio's legacy, as it turns out?" she ventured logically.

"No, he simply took advantage of what was already here. If anything, the plan he had was more easily executed because of the climate within the Vatican. If there had been more true spirituality and less—"

He glanced at Sarah.

"I feel so strange just now. I feel rather like a poor soul who has glimpsed an image of himself in hell and feels that it is not a delusion but a prophecy."

Sarah listened carefully to this man whom she had spent years hating. . .now someone she pitied greatly.

"Think of the heritage," he muttered, "After Christ ascended, Peter was to be the rock upon which this church would be built, the rock upon which it would stand. For centuries, that was the case. Now, imagine how ashamed the apostle must be if he can look down and see what we have made it from the humble beginnings he handed to future generations."

The pontiff was quiet for several minutes after that, and so was Sarah. Only a knock at the door interrupted.

He wiped his eyes and stood.

"I must see what they want," he told her. "Stay where you are."

Adolfo walked slowly to the door and opened it, every movement bespeaking the gravity of his position.

"Gervasio wants to see you," an aide told him. "He says it is urgent. I thought of not bothering you, but I realized I did not have that right."

"Do you believe him?" Adolfo asked.

The younger man, several inches shorter than he, acknowledged, "I used to believe everything he said."

"What about now?"

"I look forward to the day when I shall not have to think about him at all."

Adolfo nodded in agreement, finding that kind of forthrightness a fresh breeze carrying with it some modicum of hope.

"Tell him I will have someone with me," he replied.

"As you wish, holy father."

Adolfo had started to close the door when the aide

asked, "Am I to let him know the identity of this person?"

"Tell him only that it will be a surprise."

"As you wish, holy father."

"I am not your—" Adolfo began, but stopped.

"Pardon me, Your Holiness?" the young man asked.

The pontiff managed a half-smile.

"Nothing, Adrian. Never mind."

After Adolfo had shut the door, he asked Sarah if she had heard.

"I did, and I will go with you," she said.

"I was speaking hastily. You need not. If I were you, I could not face him for fear of becoming enraged."

"Is rage forbidden?"

"No, I suppose it is not, if it is righteous."

"Against a man like that, could it be otherwise?"

"No. . ." he said, smiling. "I will send someone for you."

"Fine. . .and thank you, Pierre Roger."

"I had not dared to dream of the daughter of Cyril Fothergill saying anything like that to me in a meeting such as this."

"Nor had I dared to dream I would be saying it."

"But how did you know that used to be my name?"

"Your brother."

"Maximillian?"

"No, your brother Henry."

"I used to think of him as poor, poor Henry, my pity crowding out even my love—when I had time to think about him at all."

"So did my father at first."

"What changed his view?"

"Your brother's purity of spirit."

Adolfo leaned against the door.

"And the meek shall inherit. . ." he whispered. "Perhaps Henry should be where I am. Perhaps he would make a better pope than I and some of those less-than-worthy predecessors I would not have difficulty identifying."

He smiled at Sarah and added, "There is something else I must say."

Sarah waited patiently.

"The fortress?" Adolfo said.

"It was a revelation," she told him honestly. "How truly remarkable the man who planned it must be."

"The nobleman who owns it, you mean?"

"Yes. . .I was hoping to meet him, tell him how wonderful it is of him to maintain the fortress as a sanctuary."

"Unfortunately you will never have that opportunity."

"He is not making himself available?"

"He cannot."

"Is he dead?"

"Yes, he is dead. He died about five years ago. In England, his home country."

"I thought he was French."

"That was part of the charade. He wished no recognition for his deed, never wanting to wring any selfish or aggrandizing motives out of it."

Adolfo smiled more broadly.

"Have you no idea, Sarah?"

"About who he—?"

Five years ago. . .in England.

An interesting coincidence occurred to her.

"That was when my grandfather—" Sarah said musingly, the truth suddenly hitting her.

She looked at Adolfo for confirmation and saw him smile more broadly, then the pontiff shut the door behind him, and left her alone, to think about her grandfather and to pray before getting ready to meet the ratman.

Adolfo took Sarah on what could be considered the long way around, and demanded that no one follow them. One of the cardinals stationed at the Vatican protested but was sent back to his quarters with a reprimand that could not be contravened.

"Such beautiful artwork!" Sarah exclaimed. "What I have heard about since I was a child is not what I see here. There is so much more. No one exaggerated."

"I am responsible for the greater part of what you see," Adolfo told her. "On my travels I would glimpse paintings, statues, rare gems, and I would either buy them or persuade the owner to donate them to the church. Always, of course, for the glory of God."

He asked her to stop briefly.

"Think of what I just said," he commented.

" 'For the glory of God,' yes."

"But how is He being glorified? Many people walk this same route through St. Peter's, but they are a very small portion of the total number of Catholics, not to mention Jews and others. How is Jehovah being glorified now? Is what I have done actually for the glory of God or the awe of men?

"And, now, today, with the hantavirus killing millions, the visitors say little when they arrive here, but I can see them looking at the treasures throughout this building, not like they used to when none felt guilty about opulence. Then they return to their countries with rotting, maggot-infected corpses blocking the streets of major cities."

He held out his hands almost in a benedictory gesture.

"I craved beautiful things before I ever knew Gervasio," he admitted, "but he did nothing to mitigate my excesses. He encouraged them."

"To weaken you spiritually," Sarah offered.

"Oh, he was most expert at that. He would make sure that beautiful women would parade through these hallways."

"How could he get away with that?"

"They would be the wives of key governmental officials or the least unsavory actresses from the traveling troupes. And he always made sure that I met each one. He never missed. I saw every one of them. I sometimes dreamed—"

He saw that she did not seem shocked.

"I have dreamed of men that way," she told him, "but I did not have someone like Gervasio constantly tempting me into lustful thoughts. It must have been worse for you."

"It was, my young friend; it surely was. I have been isolated for so long that the temptation seemed very real to me. Scripture says that thinking lustful thoughts is the same as committing an act of lust, and I have done so again and again, with Gervasio standing in the shadows, knowing that he has been successful."

She knew he had not admitted this to anyone else.

How could you? Sarah thought. *You are a symbol of holiness. You are the emissary of Jesus Christ.*

"I fought it with Louis," she told him.

He saw her framed in fleeting rays of sunlight that shone through a window behind her just before dusk.

"You were going to petition me to marry the two of you in St. Peter's Square, were you not?" Adolfo asked.

"How did you learn that?"

"Brother Thaddeus told me. He overheard the two of you talking."

Adolfo smiled as he added, "I talked to him about something in your regard, and he thought you would be pleased."

"About what?"

He reached out and took her hands in his own.

"Having a burial service for Captain Louis Dafoe in the square."

Sarah blinked several times.

"But he is a commoner, not some important—" she started to say, wondering if she had misunderstood since so much of her mind was still focused on Louis and her parents, especially now that she was soon going to come face-to-face with the most evil individual Cyril Fothergill had ever met. "I mean, Louis was hardly what you would call—"

"Shush, young lady. I am in charge here. Any rules that are not theological in nature are within my province to make or break. Your young captain was a gallant young man. Do you know anything about his background?"

"He told me a few details," she replied. "We were looking forward to spending the rest of our lives discovering whatever else there was to know about one another."

"He was the most highly decorated soldier in the history of France," Adolfo told her, "at least as far back as the records go."

"He wore no medals."

"Apparently he appreciated receiving them but did not wear any because that would have set him apart from his men far too much. Louis Dafoe believed that being a good soldier meant being a good member of a well-developed team."

"My dearest love. . ." Sarah whispered. "How can I endure losing him?"

"Loss is part of what we all endure in this world. It is one of the results of sin. There is no way of escaping it. We all face tragedy of one sort or another. For you, it has been the deaths of the four people who meant the most to you. You feel anchorless now. For others, it is the loss of their eyesight or their hearing or perhaps the loss of a limb. Are you going to tell me you would have preferred not to know such a man at all?"

"I wonder if that would have been better. It certainly would have been easier."

"You must never entertain such a notion," Adolfo scolded her sharply. "Think of how enriched your life has been. You gained the love of someone so special the likes of him may not be known again in our lifetime, or ever, Sarah. Think of that, young woman. Think of what you will be able to tell your children a decade from now."

"But since Louis was what he was, how could any other man compare? That was what made him seem all the more remarkable. I have met a number of other men, and none seemed more than ordinary. I thought that before Louis died, and what you told me about him is hardly going to change my mind. I may not marry at all, you know. I may never be a mother. I may be alone for the rest of my life because those men I shall meet in the years ahead will seem no better than the others before Louis. Only he could—"

"Do you believe that our precious Christ Jesus wants you to be alone, Sarah? Is He so cruel as that? Do not be close-minded during whatever lies ahead for you and then one day look at the emptiness of your life and cry out, 'Lord, how could You do this to me?' "

Sarah could not respond because Adolfo had argued so well and she could see no way to dispute him.

"Think of it," he pleaded. "Leave your heart open to Christ and anyone He brings into your life."

She promised Adolfo she would.

"We have to be going. But let me tell you something else before we meet with Gervasio," the pontiff said. "The French ambassador happens to be visiting, rather providentially, I think. I asked him if there would be any problem from his country's standpoint with what I was contemplating. He could think of none. In fact, his people would be quite supportive, he said. Besides, your beloved's parents are Catholic. They would feel greatly honored."

Sarah had had very little time since Louis's death to consider his burial. It was still hard for her to think of him as being dead.

"So many people watching. . ." she said absentmindedly.

"Thousands, Sarah."

"Thousands?"

Sarah knew that Captain Louis Dafoe had not sought recognition as such. He had wanted only to work with his men and to see that they acted as a unit, a team, and that precluded anyone's individual glory. Yet in death, thousands of people he did not know would attend a funeral that no one thought would come so soon.

"I intend to deliver the eulogy myself," Adolfo remarked.

She was aware that this was not a part of the tradition of the church. Adolfo was doing something that would send ripples throughout the Vatican hierarchy. Tradition, whether Scriptural or not, was an important part of the way of life of everyone inside the church.

"Where will he be buried?"

"In a cemetery on the other side of Rome. His casket will be carried in a procession through these fabled streets. Word has it that people are coming from all over the country and from France, Switzerland, and other nations as well."

"My life used to be orderly. All of that has changed. I am afraid as I have never been afraid before."

"If I had had a daughter like you. . ." he mused, "I think I would have found another way of serving the Creator."

The two of them stayed there for several minutes, then continued on their way toward the dungeons.

The ratman was waiting.

Just before they arrived at the dungeon, a member of the Vatican Guard came running toward them.

"Your Holiness, he. . .he is gone!" the soldier babbled.

"Baldasarre Gervasio escaped?" Adolfo asked.

"No. . .he is dead."

"By his own hand?"

The guard nodded hurriedly.

Knowing the man was dead relieved Adolfo on one hand and saddened him as well, for he would be wondering for the rest of his own life if he could have been the Lord's instrument for salvation in Gervasio's life given another day or two.

"I saw him banging his head against the wall," the guard said. "Before I could stop him, he had split his temple open and the top of his skull as well."

"Was he alive when you got to him?"

"For only a moment or two, Your Holiness."

"What did he say?"

"He spoke of a life filled with ridicule from the very day he had entered the world. It was rather sad at that point, Your Holiness. But he changed quickly."

"There was more?"

"Gervasio mentioned something about his first meeting with Satan."

Adolfo tried to correct the theology of that remark.

"With a demon, you mean?"

"No, what he said was that he made contact directly with Lucifer."

Adolfo glanced at Sarah as both experienced the same sort of chill.

"And then he was gone. I heard the most terrible death rattle come from his mouth, and—"

The middle-aged veteran stopped abruptly.

"Do you hear that?" he asked.

They did.

The scratching of claws on bare rock.

"Wait here!" he said.

"We will go with you," Adolfo insisted.

"Your Holiness, please stay here, out of harm's way. Let me do what I pledged from my soul to do when I became a guardsman many years ago. Let me protect you. The Lord, I am sure, wants nothing else than that from me."

"Harm's way? What could be—?"

The pontiff's eyelids opened wide.

"Surely you are wrong! How many of them could there be? I thought they were all gone, routed out many months ago."

Slowly he recognized one of Baldasarre Gervasio's last attempts to deflect any suspicion from himself. He had made a show of having the rats destroyed. No one suspected him of keeping any of them in the large, hidden room at the far end of the vault area of the catacombs, where no one else went for fear of collapsing the ancient walls weakened by age.

"They must have been hiding," the guard told the pontiff. "Let me look. I will report to you. Please, Your Holiness, think of the young woman's safety."

Adolfo nodded as he said, "You are right."

A moment or so later, they heard the man scream in shock. Then he came rushing back to them through the narrow hallway that had been cut out of solid rock centuries before.

"I must get help," he said anxiously. "And you both have to leave."

"Rats?" Adolfo asked.

"Thousands of them, more than I have ever seen in my life."

Within half an hour, a contingent of Vatican Guards were dispatched to the dungeon area, and it was sealed off temporarily.

One by one, the men entered, advancing toward the specific "cell" where Gervasio had been kept. They expected a gory sight, what was left of his body, but that was not what they saw.

Intact.

The ratman was in a sitting position, his back leaning against the uneven rock wall that had been his means of self-execution.

Hundreds of rats were gathered around Baldasarre Gervasio, covering his lap, sitting atop his bloody head, hanging from his shoulders, sprawled down his legs.

"Now!" the leader of the Vatican Guards ordered.

First they threw in pieces of crumpled paper, sheet after sheet, hundreds of them, creating an inflammable area from one side of that section of the dungeon to the other.

The rats were obviously wary, those that were not

already on or around Gervasio's body now frenziedly trying to get close to him, as though for protection, this from the man who was interested only in using them to spread disease.

The guardsmen then threw in their torches. The paper caught fire immediately, the flames quickly spreading to Gervasio's clothing.

A screeching sound.

"Like something from hell itself!" one of the younger members of the Vatican Guard yelled.

How close to the truth he was.

CHAPTER 10

Later, as Adolfo and Sarah were sitting in a private little garden at the rear of St. Peter's, trying to calm themselves and take their minds off what had happened, he turned to her and said, "Sarah, there is something I must tell you. Only a handful of people know. But by this time tomorrow, I think, the whole world will hear."

. . .the whole world will hear.

He was visibly shaken.

"Why are you letting me know this now?" Sarah asked. "I hardly deserve any special privileges."

"You are very wrong. Look at what you have suffered just within the past twenty-four hours. And I think of your father and grandfather as well."

She could not speak, those tragedies too recent, too fresh, too overwhelming.

"It is about the epidemic and everything else that has happened from last year until this very moment," Adolfo added.

Sarah waited for him to continue.

"There was no Muslim plot," he said finally, forcing out words that seemed almost to choke him.

"No—?" she exclaimed immediately. "But my father—"

"Cyril Fothergill was being deceived, as were the rest of us."

"By whom?"

Sarah was suddenly feeling chilled, as though a block of ice had been pressed up against her body from head to foot.

"By—" Adolfo started to say, but he cut himself off.

She was not breathing as she stared at him, waiting for whatever revelation it was that he would give to her.

"Gervasio confessed the truth to me," he told her, "some of it but not all. On the way to meet you, I stumbled into the rest."

His hands were trembling. Sarah reached out and calmed them with her own.

"You need not do this," she said with great sympathy.

"It is so ghastly," he replied, tears starting down his cheeks. "Muslims have been killed or imprisoned everywhere. They are even now readying—"

Sarah knew what he was going to say.

"An invasion?" she offered. "Is that what they are planning in retaliation?"

"Yes. . .from the Middle East. . .in concert with uprisings in countries where Muslims are a minority."

"Can it be stopped?"

"I have dispatched messengers to Baghdad, Teheran, Tripoli, and elsewhere."

"Will they arrive in time?"

"I hope. . .I pray so."

"But what about the epidemic? If they invade, they will be entering areas of the worst infestation."

"That does not matter to them, dear Sarah. They have only vengeance on their minds. If they die, that is a sacrifice they are prepared to make."

Sarah was shivering.

"What could your messengers possibly tell the Muslim leaders that would change matters?" she asked.

"You have no idea. What I am about to tell you would startle anyone!"

And then, exerting a self-conscious effort to get his nerves under control, Pope Adolfo began to enlighten Sarah Fothergill in what would surely rank as the most devastating revelation of modern times.

Adolfo and the Vatican Guards had left early in the morning,
foregoing their horses, and using their most reliable automo-
biles to make the journey.

The Muslims had nothing to do with it.

Gervasio's words ripped through Adolfo's mind.

They were pawns, like everyone else on the planet.

The ratman's manner had left no doubt.

"Why am I telling you now?" Gervasio had asked the
pontiff distractedly. "Because in the darkness of the night
only moments ago, I saw the terrible beckoning flames of—"

Gervasio could not continue immediately, his pathetic
little form trembling, but then, in a little while, he would say
something that filled Adolfo not with loathing but pity.

"My mother never cared about me. I was an inconve-
nience, but as a good Catholic, she never seriously considered abortion. She drank, she smoked, she took her pills,
either out of ignorance or indifference, and so I was born the
way I was, and I have had to live as best I could, filled with
the need for revenge. That was the only way I could stop my
self-pity from driving me to take my own pitiable life."

Gervasio seemed like a child then, shivering and pale
and weak.

"The epidemic? Who is really behind it? I will tell you
now, and you will know why demons have found me to their
liking. And I will direct you to the headquarters of those
who have been following my instructions. . .only a few
miles from here."

That was when the little ratman had told Adolfo the
truth, the shocking, agonizing truth that not even the most
intelligent leader on earth had guessed and that the CIA,
KGB, Scotland Yard, and other resourceful agencies had not
been able to uncover.

"They're everywhere, you know. Every country on

every continent. . .everywhere around this rotten world!"

At first Adolfo had scoffed at Gervasio's claim, but then the ratman had forced Adolfo to cross over from skepticism to acceptance and revulsion.

"Is it not perversely logical? And now the Internet has made it possible. The Internet is the greatest evil that Satan has foisted upon humankind. It has been sugarcoated, yes, because of what some Christian ministries think they are accomplishing by using it, but their efforts are being swept into some cyberspace gutter by the dark side, the province of countless cults, pedophiles, and the ultra-right militia, all the other dangerous groups that are embracing the Internet as they train countless numbers of Timothy McVeighs, John Wayne Gacys, Jeffrey Dahmers, Ted Bundys, and others who take the Internet and use it, use it better and more effectively than all the world's ministries put together."

Gervasio lapsed into silence, and Adolfo left for his own quarters, to sit alone and sob as he had never done before.

The earth-tone building was set back from the road, almost completely shielded from sight by a thick concentration of trees. But Gervasio had been precise in his directions, and Adolfo and the guards with him had had no trouble finding it.

Captain Franco Loizzi had urged the pontiff not to put himself into danger, assuring him that the Vatican Guards would carefully check out the house first and signal back to him when it seemed safe to approach.

"The whole world is in danger!" Adolfo had replied. "I shall not cower in some corner until the way is clear."

Loizzi knew that contesting against the will of the other man would have been quite fruitless, and protocol prevented it in any case, so he did not protest further when Adolfo insisted upon following immediately behind the guards.

No sounds.

Until they were less than a yard from the building.

"What is that—?" Captain Loizzi asked.

Everyone listened, trying to identify the sound.

"Typing. . .it's computer keyboards," Adolfo declared.

"All that noise?" Loizzi replied.

"*Many* keyboards."

The pontiff leaned his head against a wall of the building, pressing his ear to the masonry.

"Murmuring and talking. . ." he added, "but mostly the other."

"Can this be anything worthwhile?" Loizzi asked impatiently.

"It is *everything,* Captain!" Adolfo assured him.

He quickly told the other men why he had wanted to find this place.

"Could they hate us so much?" Loizzi asked, stunned.

"So much, yes, and more, apparently," Adolfo whispered.

"We must break in and stop them!"

"Surely we will do that. And we must also be prepared to do something else."

"What is that?"

Adolfo was sweating, because what he had to say went against everything he had been taught the whole of his adult life, and even earlier.

"We must destroy them if they retaliate," he said.

"*Destroy* them?" the captain repeated, thinking he had not heard correctly.

"What else *can* we do, put them in a prison for the rest of their lives?"

"Must we not try?"

"Even after ten or fifteen or twenty years, can they be changed?"

"But Christianity is based upon redemption," Loizzi said in a low voice, feeling most awkward about reminding the pontiff about any point of theology.

"But Christianity also recognizes the possibility of demonic possession, does it not?" Adolfo retorted. "That may be what we have here, you know, pure—"

The sounds inside had stopped momentarily.

"Now!" Loizzi ordered. "We must go in now!"

Adolfo nodded his approval.

The guards divided up, one group at the rear of the building and another, the one with which the pontiff stayed, at the front.

The old doors broke down easily. As both groups of guards charged inside, they saw what they could not have anticipated.

Freaks. . .

At least that was what insensitive people would have called them.

Two dozen young children and teenagers, nothing normal about them, each working at a laptop computer.

And stepping out from among them was obviously the oldest of the group, a man undoubtedly in his early twenties.

His hands protruded from stumps set in the middle of his chest.

"So, you did find us!" he exclaimed. "How did you accomplish that?"

"Baldasarre Gervasio," replied Adolfo.

"Our erstwhile leader," the young man said.

"When did he stop being in charge?"

"Soon after it was obvious that we were actually intent on destroying the adult world that had made him and the rest of us what we are."

"Gervasio himself never sanctioned going that far?" Adolfo asked, surprised.

"He got a twinge of conscience, I suppose."

"But not you?"

"Never me or the rest of my family here. That's what we

are, you know, a family closer than any linked by blood ties."

He smiled crookedly as he added, "I am Aaron. I suppose I have the role of being father to the others here."

"But why did Gervasio cave in?"

"Because of you."

"Me?"

"Yes, he admired you; he loved his religion."

"And you do not. . .love religion, that is?"

"Nor admire you either."

He turned and wiggled his hands toward the others.

"We are without what you would call faith, every last one of us; at least we have no faith in divinity, though we have plenty of faith in technology. With it, we are bringing civilization to an end."

"And only you will be left?" probed Adolfo.

"How astute you are! We will survive, yes, along with every other inclâvâre like us in a hundred different locations on this planet."

"Tell me why."

"You have no idea?"

"I do, yes, but I want to hear it from you."

"Look at us!" Aaron demanded.

He walked up to someone who appeared to be reasonably normal.

"See Michael here," he said. "Now turn around, my comrade."

Adolfo and the guards saw that Michael had been born with two faces; on the back of his head there appeared the impression of a second face but without eyes, only fleshy indentations where they should have been, along with a protrusion that would have been a nose, a depression that suggested a mouth, and the faint hint of a chin.

"How could—?" Adolfo started to say but was overcome, his emotions driving him to his knees.

"A careless doctor or pharmacist, not aware of what

mixing different kinds of drugs would do to a pregnant woman," Aaron explained. "And that same woman blithely drinking alcohol and smoking tobacco as she took these carelessly prescribed pills. What hope did Michael have?"

And then he walked over to another child.

"This is Roberto," he said. "He was born with part of his brain missing. He helps us as best he can, and we take care of him in return."

Adolfo saw a youngster who had trouble holding his head up, and was constantly drooling.

"What can he do for you?" the pontiff asked.

"He sings," Aaron replied.

"Sings—!"

"Listen. . . ."

The twenty-year-old asked Roberto to sing a song, any song that came to mind.

"Where is the music?" Adolfo protested. "Surely he can memorize nothing."

"Listen!"

Without accompaniment, Roberto sang so beautifully that Adolfo could think only of angels in a heavenly chorus.

"My God. . . ." he muttered.

"The pope taking God's name in vain," Aaron said mockingly. "My, oh my!"

"It was a prayer. You should know that."

"I know nothing except that I hate you and your kind, those priests who take us in and destroy our innocence."

"I am ashamed and angry over what you are implying, but it is a very small percentage of priests who commit this sin against God's children."

"You are wrong!" Aaron declared. "It is much more widespread. You have closed your mind to the truth. But even if the number of priests is small, the problem becomes immense when the priests are added to the parents who abuse us, who practice incest against us, who punish us when we step out of line while they get away with adultery, alcohol, drugs, anything they want—imposing standards of morality on us that they flaunt so brazenly!"

His rage was building.

"What protection do we have?" he demanded. "If we lift the lid on what is happening, we are thrown into the child welfare system. Is that any improvement? They shift us from foster home to foster home, and we must live with people who don't care about us at all, strangers paid to take care of us. Sometimes, they molest us. Sometimes, they beat us.

"Tell me, will you: Where do we turn? Ah, yes, to the church no doubt you will say, to the church. Yes, but in doing so we find the priests who take us in, helpless and defenseless, and start the whole ugly business all over again!"

"So you decided to bring it all down," Adolfo asked sadly, "the world as we know it?"

A cheer arose from the youngsters in that large room.

"Yes!" Aaron shot back. "Is it any worse for us than what we had? Now, at least, my comrades and I have each other."

"You'll have everything, yes, except a normal—"

"Life?" the twenty-year-old interrupted. "Everything but a normal life, right? When was life ever normal for our kind? Was it normal for a father and a brother to seduce us? Was it normal to be born as Roberto and Michael were?"

He nodded toward the gathering of misshapen or scarred forms behind him. One child sucked in air through a hole in the middle of his face where a normal nose and mouth would have been. In, then out, then in, the sounds he made seemed to be little more than noise, but Aaron apparently understood them.

"We love one another, you know. Isn't that part of a normal life? We help one another. Isn't that normal? We cry ourselves to sleep at night as we think of the past and what we now have been driven to doing, but we do so with the knowledge that there is no other way."

He let the next words flow from his mouth like lava from an erupting volcano.

"We are more normal now than ever before, even as the world we once knew crumbles at our feet because of us!"

Adolfo thought it wise to let the twenty-year-old calm down. He shot a warning glance to the guards, and they knew he wanted them not to do anything just yet.

In a few seconds, Aaron continued. "Are you curious how we did it?" he asked.

"The epidemic?" Adolfo asked.

"Yes, of course."

"I am *very* interested."

"Everything we have achieved has been because of the Internet," Aaron explained. "It is the greatest tool we could ever have had. Using it is inexpensive, and yet we can reach our associates all over the world in seconds. No law enforcement measures can stop us. The Internet cannot be tapped like phone calls can. We have absolute freedom. We control everything!"

"But what happens now?" Adolfo asked.

"We link up with others."

"What others?"

"They're in the barrios of Los Angeles and Miami and New York City."

"Street gangs?"

"Yes, yes, yes!" Aaron said ecstatically.

"But why?"

"They become our army, our police force."

"And what about the Mafia? Why not involve them as well?"

"We thought about it. But we decided they are just another part of the Establishment. They are too patriotic."

"And the Colombians?"

"Worse. They're behind the drugs that helped to make so many of us what we are."

As he listened, Adolfo had fought tears, but he could hold them back no longer. Finally, he continued, "You said you used the Internet. Tell me more, please."

"How polite we are!" Aaron exclaimed, snickering. "We found five hundred Web sites that mentioned at least one abused or molested or drug-deformed child. And we enlisted him or her. Then those five hundred found five hundred more."

"Thousands—!" Adolfo gasped.

"Many times that. Millions."

"You cannot be right. Millions?"

"There is one other category of misfits."

"What is it?"

"Babies who were aborted alive eight, ten, twelve years ago and somehow lived. They were the most unwanted of all. Some were missing arms or legs. Others had been nearly destroyed by saline solutions."

"But how did you find them?"

"We have been building toward this ever since the Internet came into being, gathering these babies together, caring for them, raising them with love."

"But the money? You must have bribed the heads of family planning clinics."

"Yes, the money did it," Aaron acknowledged. "Fetuses are sold all the time for research in labs in the United States, elsewhere, or through black market adoption outlets. Selling them to our straw men presented no problem at all. It was as if those babies were sides of beef going to a local butcher."

Adolfo winced at that, his face turning even whiter than it had been.

"May God forgive them. . ." he muttered.

"*We* won't forgive them; you can be certain of that!"

"How did you get the money?"

Aaron laughed heartily.

"You are so dense!" he exclaimed. "We robbed banks."

"Robbed—?"

"Yes, not with guns blazing, but through the Internet. We burrowed electronically into the computer systems of banks in England, Canada, and the United States, and transferred huge sums to offshore accounts in the Caribbean, in Switzerland, and elsewhere. We could have financed another world war if we had wanted to, you know. We were responsible for the collapse of that huge bank headquartered in London a few years ago. We have hundreds of millions of dollars available to us. We can buy anything we want."

Aaron was clearly enjoying himself.

"And then we manipulated the computers of disease control centers in half a dozen countries. We had hantavirus cultures transferred. We—"

He sniffed the air.

"That smells like—!" he started to say.

"Burning wood, yes, it is," Adolfo said. "You cannot be allowed to continue this infamy, whatever the cause. Come with us now, back to the Vatican. We can help you. We can—"

"Help us?" Aaron spoke with contempt. "Help us live without pain? We are too far gone for that. Help us forget our need for revenge? But that is what has kept most of us alive."

"God's love can do the same."

"Where was God's love when we were born into this world of tears? His love comes too little, too late for any of us."

"Then we must destroy you."

"Is that your punishment? You think death is so terrible a fate for the likes of us? Maybe death is the only way we can vanquish torment once and for all."

"But death for you, unless you repent, guarantees only torment for eternity," Adolfo said with passion.

"So *you* say!" the twenty-year-old retorted. "How do you

know we are not possessed and therefore are not responsible for our actions?"

Adolfo had assumed that that was the case before he and the Vatican Guards entered the building.

But now—

"I have seen many possessed of foul spirits," he answered, "and having heard you, I know the truth."

"What *is* the truth, as you see it?" Aaron asked, his voice quivering just a bit.

"That you are mentally ill, that demons have nothing to do with your condition, because they could not make you more evil than you already are!"

Adolfo knew the risks he was taking by confronting the twenty-year-old in that manner, but there seemed no other choice.

No sounds came now from any of the children or their leader.

. . .demons. . .could not make you more evil than you already are!

"We are not enslaved to Satan then?" asked Aaron.

"Not directly, no, because you served him well enough on your own, and he and the rest of his fallen ones could be elsewhere, creating other kinds of havoc."

Adolfo smiled comfortingly.

"That means you still have free will," he said.

"Free will. . . ."

Aaron seemed to be turning these two words around in his mind as though he were a jeweler examining some rare diamond for flaws.

"Is that why you have gotten deeper and deeper into this nightmare?" Adolfo asked. "You thought you could not pull free?"

"I thought—"

Aaron shook his head frantically.

"What does it matter?" he cried. "Look at the blood on

our hands!"

He moved those stubby little hands of his in an especially pitiable way.

"I could never get them clean!" Aaron exclaimed. "I could never—"

"Yes, millions of people are dead because of you and the others," the pontiff agreed, "but you would have been just as cursed if there had been only one victim. Or you would have remained unredeemed if you had not been responsible for any deaths but, rather, had simply lied or cheated or stolen. One sin alone can send you to hell."

"But what about those who kicked us, beat us, involved us in incest? What about the deformities they heaped upon us, the—?"

Adolfo spoke with as much genuine tenderness as he could muster, given that he was with perhaps the most brutal mass murderers in the history of humankind. "They will be dealt with by God," he said simply.

He paused, his eyelids narrowed, then added, "Do you want to end up in hell side by side with your abusers?"

Aaron shivered and fell to his knees. Most of the children started weeping.

"All this sin. . . ." Aaron muttered pathetically.

"Forgiven," Adolfo said softly, "even forgotten by Almighty God."

"Forgotten?"

"Yes, son, as though none of it had ever happened."

Those born with arms or hands reached their limbs out toward the pontiff. Others simply turned toward him, their eyes wide and glistening with tears.

"Help us. . ." one said. Her words were immediately joined by another's, and another's, until those two words rippled repeatedly throughout the gathering.

But Adolfo knew that unless their leader agreed the others would not continue their conversion.

He stepped closer to Aaron, placed one hand on the twenty-year-old's shoulder and reached the other down toward his chest.

"Take my hand," Adolfo asked of him. "We will go through this together."

"Yes, yes," Aaron said. "I need someone to help me. I don't know what to do. I see only a sea of faces, pale faces, all of them accusing me, all of them—"

"We will ask the Heavenly Father to wash all of that away by the shed blood of Jesus Christ, a crimson flow that will make you clean again."

And so it was, in that isolated building, in the early morning of that day, that redemption came and hell was denied those young, tormented souls.

Sarah could not speak immediately after Adolfo had finished telling her the story, but when she could, minutes later, she asked him simply, "What did you do with those children?"

"I had some of the Vatican Guards take them back to St. Peter's, and then the rest of us continued on to meet up with you," he told her.

"How did you find out about us?"

"Captain Dafoe had radioed in about what was going to happen."

"My dear Louis."

"He will be honored as he should be, and your sister as well."

She reached out, and they held one another for a very long time.

CHAPTER 11

Louis Dafoe, captain in the army of the country of France, and Clarice Fothergill were given a funeral that drew people from half a dozen countries and a variety of religions: Catholics, Jews, Hindus, Buddhists, and most controversially, Muslims.

Ten thousand men and women filled St. Peter's Square surrounding the two extraordinary caskets that had been placed in the exact middle, Louis's body in the one on the left and Clarice's on the right. Those who lived closer to the Vatican had heard a great deal about the young captain over the past two days; nor was Clarice unknown either, if only because of Cyril Fothergill, her father, and because of Raymond Fothergill, her grandfather, both of whom had become the stuff of budding folklore that would acquire a life of its own and continue on for perhaps centuries.

But Adolfo had to face something of a quandary. He had gotten permission from the French ambassador to bury a French citizen on Italian soil. However, there was no time to contact Prime Minister Edling regarding a British citizen. It was Sarah who had to approve this, and she did so without distress.

"If either my father or my mother were yet alive, I would have to consult them," she pointed out, "but they are not, and so it falls to me."

"Remember," Adolfo said objectively, "your heritage is in England. All the other members of your family, going back centuries, I assume, are buried on English soil."

"Are you suggesting it is improper?" she asked.

"Only you can decide that. . .since no one older is left to make the decision for you."

"Then I ask that you go ahead. And if my conscience later assails me, I shall have to deal with it then. For now there seems no choice."

So arrangements were made, and two days later, the service began. Pope Adolfo I gave the eulogy, not from the balcony high above the front entrance, but as he walked among those in the crowd. His advisors had argued against this, citing the possibility that he would be an open target for anyone who was anti-Catholic.

"I have been separated from the people far too long," he told them. "That is not what Christ intended, nor was it what He practiced. The crowds went with Him wherever He was and surrounded Him at every step. Can I do less? Have I paid more attention to my own safety than to the well-being of millions of believers?"

"But this is a time of plague," one of them persisted. "You could become contaminated. Have you considered that, Your Holiness?"

"To die doing the will of my blessed Savior, what a blessing to be bestowed by the Father above, dear man!" Adolfo answered. "How can I shrink from that like a man with no hope of heaven? Is this life so precious that we cannot lose it for Him as He gave His own up for you, me, and all those who would accept Him into their very souls?"

They relented. Once the pope spoke, no one dared oppose him.

And so he walked among the thousands, telling them of Louis Dafoe's bravery and his sacrifice.

"He died that a little baby might live," Adolfo spoke. "He had no thought for himself but that one life, the least of God's creation. Let part of the legacy of Louis Dafoe be the respect we maintain for the life of our young, born or unborn; there is no difference. Let us be willing to sacrifice for our children, even if it means giving up our own lives."

He turned first in one direction, then another.

"I have been, as Christ's vicar, foolish in listening to the wrong voices, but no longer. Let that be another part of the legacy of this young man."

And then he turned his attention to Clarice, speaking of her loyalty to her sister and her faith in God and reminding the onlookers of the other Fothergills, Cyril and Raymond.

"In an age where selfishness is rampant, Clarice seldom put her own welfare first. She was eager to return to England, not so much to escape the plague but to see her parents before they died. Then, when she learned that her father was dead, she thought, again, not of herself but of her mother, wanting to comfort Elizabeth Fothergill.

"This was the sort of family, whether rich or poor, upon which Christian culture is based. And it should be an example to all of us. Only through the family, rooted in the historic Christian faith, can civilization as we know it survive."

A young man fell down in front of him.

"I have done so much to be ashamed of, holy father!" he said. "I do not know if I have the strength to give up sin as this man must have done, as that young woman surely did."

"Louis was not sinless; nor was Clarice, I am sure," Adolfo corrected him. "None of us are. What these two did was not let their sin nature rule them. Louis, in a moment of the most extreme danger, did not give in to cowardice or fear or selfishness and consider himself above a helpless infant."

"But how can I ever compare?"

"You never can. . .by yourself. Let the Holy Spirit take over, and you will soar like an eagle."

"If only I could."

"If only you *will!*"

The young man disappeared back into the crowd.

More men and women took advantage of this rare opportunity, which few would have had otherwise, to speak directly to Pope Adolfo. Kings and queens and statesmen and wealthy landowners, yes, but seldom was the pope exposed to the words of the common people who, if they saw him at all, did so as he stood on his balcony and blessed them.

From such a distance they had developed a way of spreading what he was saying to those who could not possibly hear him. They whispered his words to others, and so they went, on and on across the square, until no one was unaware of what the pontiff was saying.

He finally reached the caskets that had been placed on a raised wooden platform. And remarkable caskets they were, with solid gold adornments in the shape of angels covering the entire top of each one. The wood had been imported from India.

Sarah was waiting for him there.

So were Brother Thaddeus and Brother Nathaniel, along with Monique Dumelle and the men of Louis's troop who had accompanied them from the fortress to Rome. All of the members of that little group had been waiting on the platform beside the caskets since before the crowd had gathered.

Adolfo walked around the stage, talking to the crowd in as loud a voice as he could muster, though it was already acquiring a slightly hoarse edge.

"Louis's loyalty to his men is akin to Christ's love for us, as was Clarice's loyalty to Louis and to her sister, Sarah. Is it not so that to those we love, to them we pledge our loyalty? Is there love without loyalty? Is not loyalty without love something cold and empty, something that can shift as easily as sand on a Mediterranean beach?"

One of the hardened soldiers over whom Louis had had command started weeping audibly. Another soon followed.

"That is the sound of love," Adolfo told the crowd. "It is not weak for men of valor to shed such tears. It is not weak for them as men to love another. Louis Dafoe's sacrifice arose from that love. Duty alone would never have served."

He touched his own cheeks and found them wet.

"I cry for the millions who have died of the epidemic. If we think only of ourselves, of what violent acts we must commit to survive as long as the plague thrives among us, there is no hope, for the reward of selfishness is the death of whatever good remains in the human spirit."

Adolfo paused, clearing his throat, and then went on, little of what he said rehearsed.

"Many hundreds of years ago, a wise Roman philosopher said that he who lives only for himself is truly dead to others. We can survive the plague physically but be dead spiritually if we allow our sin to be manipulated by Satan, with no concern for those who exist beyond the walls of our own homes."

"But I will not allow the disease to be spread to any members of my family!" someone declared. "I must keep them and myself free of contamination. How can I love my neighbor and be kind to him if he has the plague?"

"Can you bake some bread and deliver it to the doorstep of a sick family?" Adolfo asked.

"Yes. . .of course."

"You tell them not of your apprehension by acting in this way but of your love instead. Will you do that? Will you do that as soon as you return home?"

"Yes, holy father. . .praise God, I shall!"

"And if they and you survive, you will be bonded together as friends for life, because you must not stop with one loaf of bread. Do you know this, my brother?"

"I will give them eggs and cheese and whatever else I can spare."

Adolfo smiled and told the one who had spoken, "Go to your home and then to your neighbor, and do as you have said."

Suddenly, the crowd gasped.

A representative of the Muslims had been standing near the entrance to St. Peter's, conspicuously isolated from the other dignitaries.

Without warning, he walked down the steps toward the crowd, which parted to let him pass. He was a regal-looking man, well over six feet tall, slender, with a nose so long it looked almost comical. Atop his narrow head was an elaborate turban, crisscrossed with diamonds and emeralds.

"I am Fawwaz Telal Meshkur," he said in a voice that was clear and resonant, carrying farther into the throng than Adolfo's.

The people who formed the crowd, though they had let him pass, were transparently hostile. No one there was ignorant of the Muslim plot, and all were being affected by its perverse success.

"I have come here to give homage to Captain Louis Dafoe," he proclaimed.

"Why else?" the pontiff asked. "Are we to believe that the death of one man has beckoned you to Rome?"

"There is a second reason, the opportunity for it provided by the first."

"You interrupt this funeral to spread propaganda?"

"I interrupt this funeral to beg Christian forgiveness."

"Forgiveness? For—?"

"For epidemic that has caused the deaths of millions of Europeans."

There was the suggestion of a wry smile curling up the sides of Meshkur's mouth.

"For not cooperating with you and helping to find those responsible. Only within the past twenty-four hours have we learned the truth."

No one spoke for a moment. Not a word was uttered in the crowd nor from Adolfo or the monks or any of the soldiers. It was Sarah who finally broke the silence.

"My father is dead because of the epidemic," she said. "Perhaps he might be alive today if you had helped us. Millions of Muslims might have been able to find the truth before the hantavirus had spread so far."

Meshkur whipped out a curved dagger.

"Would my own death help?" he asked.

"But you are innocent of what others have done," Sarah told him.

"If by my death all the horror could be wiped out, I would die gladly."

"Put your weapon away," Adolfo spoke up. "Only the death of Christ was sufficient for all."

The Muslim fell to his knees before Adolfo.

"Then tell me how to become a Christian, and I shall."

"Out of guilt? Is that why? You want to have your guilt washed away by the shed blood of a Christian Savior?"

"That is all I have left."

Adolfo grabbed him by the shoulders.

"Stand, then. After the funeral, I shall personally lead you to Jesus."

Meshkur had dropped the dagger and was standing now, smiling through tears that had started to flow.

"To be free of this awful shame!" he exclaimed. "What a glorious—"

Suddenly his tone contorted, and he fell forward, against Adolfo.

Someone from the crowd had pushed through and picked up Meshkur's dagger and jabbed it into the Muslim's back.

"For my wife!" the bearded assailant screamed. "For my sons, my daughters!"

He was starting to lift the dagger once again when someone else from the crowd grabbed his wrist and forced him to drop it. But another man picked it up and plunged it into Meshkur's side.

Adolfo tumbled to the ground with the weight of the Muslim on top of him.

"He is attacking the holy father! He is—" shouted a voice nearby. "Stop him!"

Meshkur's first attacker pushed his way back through the crowd and tried to flee the scene. But he would not get far, for the Vatican Guardsmen stationed around St. Peter's Square were after him.

Adolfo's white robe was splotched with blood.

One of the guardsmen rushed up to him and said, "We must get you inside. There must be others. And you have to be cleaned up."

"You must not do anything of the sort," he said. "This young captain's funeral must proceed without further interruption."

"But Your—" the soldier protested.

"I am about the business of honoring the courage of Louis Dafoe," Adolfo retorted. "Shall I play the part of a coward myself?"

The crowd calmed down.

Papal physicians had rushed outside. Adolfo instructed them to care for Fawwaz Telal Meshkur until he finished the service. Then he would pray with the man as he accepted Christ as Savior and Lord.

The funeral proceeded, and when the ceremony ended, the procession slowly filed out of St. Peter's Square, past the Marmetine Prison where the apostle Paul had been confined prior to his execution, then a right turn along one side of the Forum and through the ancient streets of Rome to a little cemetery on the outskirts of the city.

By then the number of onlookers had grown from the original ten thousand to thrice that many. Only Pope Adolfo, Sarah, Brother Thaddeus, Brother Nathaniel, Monique Dumelle, and the French soldiers who had served with their captain were allowed inside the cemetery's wrought iron fence, for wont of room.

At the grave sites, Adolfo delivered a brief homily; then he walked to the fence and repeated it to the larger crowd.

"And now I have to be returning to St. Peter's," he told

them. "A brother needs the Good News that has been entrusted to me."

Nearly thirty thousand men and women made the sign of the cross and then went their way.

Sarah hesitated beside the graves, kneeling between the two.

Adolfo returned to her side for a moment.

She heard him approach and looked up.

"So many years with Clarice," she said, her voice breaking.

"Walk with me now?" he asked.

"Yes, I will."

"I will have you on your way tomorrow with an armed contingent of Vatican Guards."

One of Louis's men overheard and asked for permission to speak.

"Could we do that, Your Holiness?" he asked.

"Take Sarah home?"

"Yes, it would be an honor, and it does seem appropriate in view of the fact that she and our captain would have been husband and wife by now."

Adolfo thought for a moment, then agreed.

"I think two of my guards should also be present."

"May I ask why?" the French soldier spoke, bristling a bit.

"A group of French soldiers arriving on English soil?" Adolfo replied without elaboration.

"Of course. I was not thinking."

Sarah wondered when danger caused by epidemic or politics would be vanquished from her life.

Or will it be there, in some form, she thought, *until my loved ones and I walk the golden streets together?*

The journey up to the northern end of Italy and then across France provided a panorama of life in an era of plague. The horror was every bit as vivid as Sarah had assumed, given

the capsule views she had had while heading toward the
fortress, especially as she traveled the far greater expanse of
land through the central part of the country.

And then there were the wizards, men who had been
traveling the roads of Europe selling holy water and crucifixes
and magic spells. Eventually Adolfo railed against them,
removing any blessing upon their activities that might have
been implied by the Vatican's previous silence, engineered
as it was by Baldasarre Gervasio. But even that did not stop
them, for as the death toll mounted, hitting twenty million,
twenty-one million, and increasing to thirty million men,
women, and children, with a disproportionate percentage
those adults who were elderly and already weakened by the
encroachments of age, understandably panicking Europeans
became ever more desperate for relief, and the wizards were
more compelling than the far-off voice of even the pope himself. They offered protection for a price, forgiveness-on-the-
spot, and they were patently evil, these strange men in their
often bizarre clothes that made them look either like court
jesters at one extreme or funeral directors at the other.

But then the little caravan reached the seaport, where
their ship was being readied for more passengers than it
usually accommodated, creating worse conditions for the
crew as the French soldiers and the two members of the
Vatican Guards were crowded into their quarters. The ship's
captain gallantly gave up his cabin for Sarah and offered to
bunk with his crew.

Then the only task left to Sarah was saying good-bye
to those who had entered her life and affected it so deeply,
Brother Thaddeus and Brother Nathaniel. Their parting occurred on a dock overlooking the English Channel, the odor
of fish and salt water in the air, and the sound of gulls over-
head.

And then Sarah was aboard a vessel not unlike the one
on which her father had traveled during his fateful journey.

CHAPTER 12

The English Channel was calm during the entire trip.

"My father faced the most violent storms each time," she remarked.

"But look at what the whales did," Vatican Guardsman Alberto Liberatore reminded her. "They must have been provided by the Lord Himself."

"I always thought that. What else could their purpose have been? To show off how intelligent whales are?"

She had no need of help on this crossing, at least not the kind those whales could have provided. There was no storm at sea, and no telltale shark fins could be glimpsed.

Even so, just before the ship's anchor was dropped off-shore at the white cliffs, Sarah thought, as she stood on the deck, that she could detect something in the distance, a black-and-white shape rising up out of the water, but then it sank and was gone, and she decided it must surely have been her imagination. . . .

Sarah had seen the white cliffs upon her return from each of the vacations she had taken with Clarice. But she had usually looked upon them with a mixture of homecoming and regret, glad that she was back but sorry to have to break away from the undeniable good times she and her sister had always enjoyed in Switzerland.

Liberatore stood on the weathered old deck with her, alternately joining Sarah in conversation or letting her talk by herself or simply taking in the scents that seaborne breezes carried.

In less than half an hour, the ship's captain would order

that the anchor be dropped.

"I wish I could go with you," he told her. "It would mean a great deal to me to stand at your father's grave and pay my respects. He was so fine a man. I could not think more highly of my own father."

Sarah did not immediately reply but closed her eyes as a pounding sensation at her temple distracted her.

"Have I offended you in some way?" Liberatore asked after a moment.

"You have not. . ." Sarah told him. "I was just reminded that I could not be at his side when he died. That is the hardest part, you know. I wish I could have held his hand and kissed him and told him how much I loved him."

"It was different with my father," Liberatore replied. "He took part in the Gulf War. The Iraqis captured him when he was wounded and unable to retreat. They cut him into little pieces and fed them to wild dogs."

He had tried to hide any show of emotion from what he was saying.

"Excuse me," he said. "Here I am—"

Sarah brushed the fingers of her right hand across his cheek.

"You need not feel awkward," she told him. "We are not stoics after all. There is no Greek in my blood."

"There's a little in mine," he said. "That may be why shedding tears in front of a lady when her own troubles—"

"Shush!" she said. "We can talk about something else if you like or not talk at all. But if you want to continue, that is fine with me. I recoil from very little these days."

He shook his head and told her that he had not spoken in years about what happened to his father.

"There is nothing more," he said, "just the emptiness I feel when I think of him."

He wiped his eyes.

"My father had no illusions about human nature,"

Liberatore said. "He had some feeling that men who were devils would kill him someday. We never knew why he felt that way, but he did."

The captain's voice could be heard shouting, "We drop anchor now. Everyone at their stations. It seems there is quite a welcoming party waiting for us."

Sarah and Alberto Liberatore had been at the seaward end of the vessel as it docked. Though neither admitted it openly at first, they were hoping to catch some glimpse of a school of killer whales swimming near them.

When the call to drop anchor came, they glanced at one another and laughed.

"After all, they are hardly that intelligent," Sarah spoke for both of them.

And then they hurried toward the bow.

The captain was not exaggerating.

Sarah could count twenty people on the beach, plus assorted limousines, two regular sedans as well as a motorcycle, and two very conspicuous royal carriages.

"I can scarcely believe it!" she exclaimed.

"Whom do you see?" Liberatore asked.

"The prime minister is here. . .and Queen Elizabeth!" she told him breathlessly, her youth showing. "The queen herself is right there on shore, with an entourage of members of the royal court."

"I wonder what is going on?" Liberatore asked, impressed.

She could have told him, but it would have sounded arrogant, and so she said nothing in response, knowing that her father had been a man respected above most others, and it would have surprised her if there had been no one at all waiting on the beach.

Yet seeing the queen did take Sarah aback. She could not have anticipated her presence.

The ship's captain, a younger man than most, came up

to them and said, "It is time. They are sending a small boat for you. May I get your possessions?"

Sarah realized that she had nothing with her but the few items of clothing she had salvaged from the chalet in Switzerland.

"Give them to the needy," she told the captain.

"My wife and I are quite poor," he replied.

"Take everything," Sarah urged. "How long will you be here?"

"Just two or three days. I have someone to pick up in London and a cargo of goods to load, and then I am gone."

"Where can I reach you?"

He gave her the address.

"I shall have some other clothes and some additional items sent to you."

"You are so kind, m'lady. I deserve none of this."

"Let me try very hard to make life for you and your family a little easier. That would be my pleasure, Captain."

The man thanked her then pointed to the little boat that was pulling up beside his ship.

"I shall be sorry to have you go," Liberatore said. "Someday perhaps you will be able to see my family."

"I would like that."

"May I help you into the boat?" the captain asked.

"I will do that," Liberatore said.

The captain nodded and left.

"I was so blessed to know your father," Liberatore told her.

"We all were," she said. "Everywhere I go in our home, I will see him in my mind, his words coming back to me from all the memories of the twenty-odd years he and I had together."

"And your mother? She must have been a fine woman to have raised such a daughter."

"No one spoke ill of her because they would have to

spend only a short while with her to know that she was special. She had no desire beyond the welfare of those she loved."

Trying not to give in to tears, Sarah attempted to change the subject.

"You would have liked my sister, Clarice, as well."

"I feel I know her."

"You do?"

"Your father spoke a great deal of the two of you. He was proud of you both."

She turned and looked at those awaiting her.

"I know none of them," she said forlornly. "How can they do anything but remind me that my loved ones are gone, or else they would not be waiting for me now?"

"But you will be surrounded by people, kind people, over the next few weeks. Should you resist them? Shouldn't you let our good Lord speak to you through them?"

She was glad that he felt free enough to talk to her in that manner.

"Thank you, Alberto. You have helped. Keep me in your prayers."

"I will, of course, and the holy father will not forget your needs, either."

She put her arms around him. He was a bit older than Louis had been but pleasant enough to be with, and if their respective circumstances had been different, she could have allowed herself to become very fond of him.

Liberatore helped Sarah over the side and into the little boat that would take her to shore.

"Good-bye," he called out, waving.

She waved back to him and smiled.

"May God bless your journey home," she said.

"And yours the rest of the way, Sarah Fothergill."

I am so tired, she thought as she watched sadly, *so tired of saying good-bye.*

She turned toward those familiar white cliffs looming

just beyond the beach where her parents had regularly taken her and Clarice as children to make castles in the sand and swim in the Channel or watch birds swoop down to snatch a catch of sole from the clear water.

Sighing, Sarah Fothergill readied herself to face the kindness of strangers.

Prime Minister Harold Edling stepped out into the cold water of the English Channel and personally carried Sarah to shore.

"Are you surprised that someone such as I would do this?" he asked, rather proud that he had ignored expectations so brazenly.

"Very surprised, sir," she replied, smiling brightly.

As soon as he put her down on dry sand, people gathered around her, prepared to meet every need that she had.

"They are so willing to help," she whispered to Edling.

"And that willingness comes from the heart," he told her. "None of them want anything from you, Sarah."

"Not even to take over the management of the Fothergill estate?" she said but apologized instantly. "That was uncalled for, sir. I am weary, and my manners flee."

"You are quite right, actually," Edling acknowledged, "but not regarding these people. That other crowd, the one you describe so accurately, will descend upon you a few days after you have reestablished yourself at home. And even they would not do so right away, for then they would show themselves to be what they are: vultures. Depend upon encountering a facade of fawning sympathy, Sarah, but do not be deceived by it."

"But how will I protect myself? How can I make sure that everything my parents strove for will be maintained?"

"You are going to have the protection afforded by the power of my office!" Edling declared.

"And mine!" Queen Elizabeth said as she walked regally

up to the two of them. "What more protection could you want, my dear?"

"But surely you have many more important—"

"You must never think that," the queen interrupted, an unusual act for someone well-versed in social and diplomatic etiquette. "Your father and your grandfather wanted only what was right and proper for those they loved."

Sarah turned her attention to the group of men and women who had come along because their prime minister and their queen had wished it. Contrary to a fleeting notion that they must all be strangers, Sarah discovered that she had met several of them at banquets given by her father and was able to remember their names, which charmed them greatly.

"What a remarkable young woman!" a well-dressed, middle-aged, plumpish woman exclaimed, then added mischievously. "Do you remember how many children I have?"

"Five," Sarah told her, "three boys and two girls, Lady Collinsworth."

The other woman giggled and then blushed.

"I am sorry," she said, "this is not a time for levity."

"It is very hard for me now," Sarah added. "I wonder how I will stand the next few days or weeks or—"

Lady Collinsworth abruptly shed any pomposity and held Sarah's hands.

"While you were gone, I lost my sons to the epidemic," she said, "and my husband. I have only my daughters left. I know what you are feeling, Sarah. Think nothing of my silliness. It is one way I have of surviving. But I do not take lightly your own tragedies. In them I see my own. If my daughters had died, too, I think I would have gone quite mad."

She leaned forward and kissed Sarah on the cheek.

"Let me help you," she said. "And my daughters would like to pitch in, you know. It is hard for all of us to stay where we have lived the greater part of our lives. We think we hear the sounds of those we loved so much, familiar voices at odd times of the day and night."

Several others introduced themselves before the queen called a halt to what was becoming an unplanned social gathering, one that went beyond anything she had intended and which she knew must be taxing Sarah's dwindling energies.

"Quite enough!" she announced but without sounding harsh.

The queen nodded toward the awaiting royal coaches.

"You will have one nearly to yourself," she said.

Queen Elizabeth simply smiled as she walked with Sarah to the first coach in line.

"I will plan on spending time with you the day after tomorrow," she said.

"You will be coming to Fothergill Castle?" Sarah asked, surprised.

"You both will need help."

"What do you mean, Your Royal Highness?"

Queen Elizabeth smiled again as she started to open the door of the coach then snapped her fingers and stepped aside.

"Your horseman will want to do that," she said. "How forgetful of me!"

Sarah was sure that something was going on, but by then she was too tired to question anything.

"Welcome home!" a cheerful voice cried out.

She spun around.

Henry Letchworth!

The two hugged.

"I thought everyone was gone," Sarah confessed. "I thought the castle would be empty, and I would do nothing but wander its bleakness day after day until I wearied of it all and. . ."

Henry rested a finger ever so gently on her lips.

"Be calm, dear Sarah," he said.

He reached for the door, then, in a now-familiar act, snapped his fingers and stepped aside.

"The other horseman wants to do it," he told her.

Now Sarah was certain that something quite strange was happening.

"Who is the other horseman?" she asked. "Who—?"

Roger Prindiville jumped off the horseman's seat and reached out for her with the only arm he had left.

"You—?" she spoke.

"I lost it fighting off some interlopers who tried to take over the castle," Prindiville said without seeming bitterness. "They took advantage of the growing chaos throughout England, but we were able to defeat them."

"They—?"

He nodded but did not elaborate, not wanting to spoil her homecoming.

"Much has happened, m'lady, so much," he said, hoping she would not question him anymore about it.

She threw her arms around him.

"I assumed there would be no one left, no one at all. But you two! Thank God you made it!"

Suddenly it was as though some hairs had moved on the back of her neck, like alerting antennae.

A voice then.

Not the queen's, or Henry's, or Roger Prindiville's, or Lady Collinsworth's, though it was a woman's voice.

From the carriage.

Almost numbly, Sarah allowed both men to help her up into it while Harold Edling held open the door.

A veiled figure sat in one of the two seats.

Abruptly, a pale hand splotched with liver marks and protruding veins snapped the veil to one side.

"Praise God!" Elizabeth Fothergill spoke with familiar tenderness as she reached out her arms. "Let me hold you, my dearest; let me do what I have begged Him to allow and what He now has seen fit to bestow."

Sarah held onto the frame of the carriage, hesitating,

numb, not quite believing what she heard, what she saw.

"Mother, you look—!" Sarah exclaimed.

"Healthy? Oh, I have become that, after a fashion. I do feel myself getting stronger in stages—or that might be wishful thinking. Who knows? Whatever the illness was that I had before you left has somehow made me, so the queen's physicians seem convinced, now immune to the hantavirus. For that alone, of course, I rejoice."

Elizabeth coughed but only briefly and did not seem under any distress otherwise.

"Everyone around me has died, but I live on. I have far more wrinkles, I know, and I need to gain some more weight. Yet I am healthy, dear, dear Sarah. I am healthy!"

Still feeling dazed, Sarah climbed into the carriage and sat down beside her mother.

"You are alive, Mother!" she exclaimed with awe. "How many times has it been that I have dreamed of—?"

"Standing by my grave? You are not alone. How many times have I dreamed of standing by yours one day and wanting to die if I had to face that vast place we call home with no one I loved behind its walls?"

"Clarice is—" Sarah started to say.

"Yes, I know. I know about my blessed child," Elizabeth said sadly.

"How did you—?"

"A special papal messenger was flown in days ago. Adolfo wanted to prepare me, and I love him for that."

Elizabeth cleared a throat suddenly clogged.

"My dear, dear Clarice," she said. "I can never see where that sweet child is buried."

"It is a beautiful little cemetery," Sarah hastened to tell her. "Trees everywhere, and roses, Mother, the most wonderfully fragrant roses."

They cried, mother and daughter, cried over one who would never be with them again in the flesh, cried until they were spent, and then managed to find more words, words that rushed forth in a torrent pent up for a very long time, talking almost all the way back to Fothergill Castle. But for those last few miles they sat in silence, the two of them, as though that moment could not be but was, looking at one another, lost in inexpressible joy.

Fic
Elwood

ELWOOD
Bright Phoenix.